I0550187

IRREVERSIBLE

BOOK SIX

THE BLOODLUST CHRONICLES

TARA VASSER

Copyright© Winter Musings LLC **2017** Copyright info: Winter Musings LLC
15310 Taylor St NE
Ham Lake, MN 55304

978-1-947882-07-2 PRINT

978-1-947882-08-9 EBOOK - MOBI

978-1-947882-09-6 EBOOK - EPUB

978-1-947882-10-2 AUDIOBOOK

Editing By: There for You Editing

Cover Art By: DuskTilDawn Designs

Photo Credit:

Royal Touch Photography

IRREVERSIBLE

IRREVERSIBLE IS THE FINAL INSTALLMENT IN THE BLOODLUST CHRONICLES. IT IS WRITTEN TO BE READ FOLLOWING ENJOYMENT OF IRRESISTIBLE (BOOK 1), IRREDEEMABLE (BOOK 2), IRREPLACEABLE (BOOK 3), IRRECOVERABLE (BOOK 4) AND IRREPRESSIBLE (BOOK 5)

DEDICATION

To Tony – Thank you for believing in me and not letting me give up, even when I wanted to.

Acknowledgements

Special thanks go out to:

Ashley for being my bestie, even when all I talk about is writing.

Jen for reminding me what Mrs. Hein taught us in ALP and applying it to my stories.

Chase, Mandy, Sammie, Roman, Johanna, and Henry for bringing my characters to life and hanging out with me for the better part of an afternoon to get all the photos for The Bloodlust Chronicles covers in one fell swoop.

Royal Touch Photography for the amazing photos. Thank you for your awesomeness

Dusk Til Dawn Designs for enduring my adjustments and setting me straight when I start to veer off into la-la-land.

Melissa for rocking my socks off and being an awesome editor.

And last, but absolutely never least—my readers. Thank you so much for sticking with me throughout The Bloodlust Chronicles. I appreciate each and every one of your support by reading my books. I hope you all will continue with me on my writing journey into new territory. Thank you so much for all you to do make this writing dream a reality!

IRREVERSIBLE

Old enemies emerge from the shadows, storming the Vampires' lab, halting testing on the preliminary formulation of the cure for Vampirism. As the twisted web of events dating back to Endre's incarceration beneath the earth begins to unravel, the Vampires learn they have merely been pawns in an elaborate revenge scheme.

When all hell breaks loose, the life of one of their own is cut short and a deadly new creature is spawned, sparking awareness of side-effects of the cure.

In a startling turn of events, unlikely allies come to the rescue, allowing the Vampires to continue their work to create a viable serum in an attempt to reverse the effects of Vampirism.

CHAPTER ONE

It was exceedingly difficult for Nora to make sense of the last several minutes. So much had gone wrong in so little time. Rodriguez was back from the dead, one of her worst fears come back to haunt her in a more dangerous form than he had been as a Hunter … a Vampire. She could only pray to whatever god would listen that she wouldn't have to taste his blood and see the new memories he'd made since his transition. She still had nightmares from what she'd witnessed in his blood as a Hunter, she could only imagine she'd never want to close her eyes again if she had to endure viewing his life as a ruthless predator. And now, they were even further outmatched with her having been injected with the serum—the cure—which was developed to turn her back into a human. It left her completely at the mercy of the sadistic beast that was Rodriguez.

Looking over at Endre, Nora wasn't sure if she would be able to decipher if he still lived if she was no longer a Vampire. She was officially their first test-subject with the serum, and had no idea what to expect.

Would the enhanced senses she'd had as a Vampire vanish immediately? Would they fade away in time? Would she merely drop dead because something had gone horribly wrong? She was surprised to find she could still hear Endre's heartbeat. And Jackson's. They were both still alive … at least for now.

Her gaze swept over to where Alicia lay in a pool of blood, her clothing smeared with it from where her sister's hands had pressed over the wound, trying to stop the flow. There was no heartbeat coming from Alicia. The other hearts surrounding her, however, seemed to be in no danger of ceasing to pump blood to their hosts, even if Nora was of the opinion they didn't deserve to.

A tight grip around Nora's neck brought her attention back to the sadistic fuck holding her captive, keeping her from running to Endre like she wished. She couldn't see Rodriguez's eyes while he held her, waiting for his next order, and for that Nora was thankful. She didn't know how long it would take once she saw into those malicious eyes for her to plummet off the precipice of the fine edge she walked between sanity and madness. When he had been a mere Hunter, looking into his eyes had been like staring Death himself full in the face. Now, a complete unraveling of her mind would accompany but a glimpse.

"Bring our little guinea pig over here," Micelli's voice ordered.

Nora's gaze snapped up to meet the man's eyes. When she'd met Dave Micelli about eight months ago she thought he was human. Up until a few minutes ago, she'd thought he was a Vampire. Now, she was sure he was entirely something else. His taunts to Alicia after she'd injected him with a syringe-full of the cure tended to indicate he was a Hunter. None of them suspected.

Unstrapping the Vampire who was *supposed* to be their first test subject for the cure from a table, Micelli beckoned Rodriguez forward. Rodriguez moved without an ounce of hesitation, bringing Nora toward her newest prison. Having spent enough time being chained and bound and strapped to things, she struggled in Rodriguez's grip. He was much too strong for her to fight off. His arm tightened around her neck and she grew lightheaded from the lack of oxygen.

A gurgling sound, followed by a thud, brought Nora's attention away from the table where she was sentenced to be strapped, to where Micelli stood. Or, where he had been standing a few moments prior. Her gaze landed on where his body convulsed on the floor. A horrific noise rose from him. Rodriguez stepped back, taking Nora with him.

"Go get that nurse!" one of the other Vampires on guard yelled.

"Leave him," the woman Alicia had called Jackie commanded from the edge of the room. Her voice had an eerie calm to it that put Nora on edge. "Let him die."

The entire room stood in stunned silence at her proclamation. Jackie took easy strides over to where

Micelli lay on the floor. Looking down at him dispassionately, she shook her head before turning to address the whole room.

"He was just a means to an end," Jackie sneered.

Nora gasped when she got a full view of the woman's face in the light. She was a dead ringer for the Vampire Endre had considered a sister. *Jaqueline.*

"Jaqueline?" Nora whispered, not having meant to say it aloud.

But it couldn't be. Jaqueline was dead, Lorenzo killed her. At least Nora assumed he had; she hadn't *actually* seen Lorenzo finish the job in the blood memory she'd witnessed. Endre had interrupted her before she could see the culmination.

"Ah, yes, you're Nora," Jaqueline spat, turning her full attention to Nora.

Hatred brewed in the woman's eyes, though Nora couldn't fathom why.

"You're alive! We thought you were dead," Nora exclaimed. "We thought Lorenzo executed you."

Jaqueline laughed, and it came out sounding like a woman on the edge of hysteria. "Is that the reason he gave for not searching me out?"

"I saw it in Lorenzo's memory. He had a gun pointed at your head …" Nora started, mildly surprised Rodriguez was allowing her to speak.

A little chuckle escaped Jaqueline. "Oh, so *you* told him Lorenzo murdered me, so he didn't come looking for me?"

"I didn't see the end," Nora placated, trying to shake her head with Rodriguez's grip still around her neck. "We just assumed you'd died."

"You know what they say about making assumptions," Jaqueline spat. "I traded Lorenzo information for my life. He thought I loved him, and I let him believe it. He shot his guards instead. The man was so proud, he didn't want anyone to know he'd shown me mercy. It all worked out in my favor, though, so I can't complain too much. I'm the one who told him Endre had been freed."

So she was the reason Lorenzo had known they were in Paris.

"And he let you go?" Nora questioned, deciding it would be better to keep Jaqueline talking if it kept her from being strapped to the table.

"He had no choice. It was either let me go, or let those around him know he showed mercy after I betrayed him." Jaqueline rolled her eyes as though the answer should have been obvious to Nora.

"You betrayed him?" Nora was genuinely curious how the other Vampire was standing before her and how this whole tale came to be.

"Yes," Jaqueline gloated with a deranged smile. "Lorenzo kept me captive. He abused me. He told me he loved me. I *hated* him. But I let him believe I loved him and he grew to trust me … after nearly ninety years as his captive. Can you even imagine the concept of being the *sex* slave of a vicious asshole like Lorenzo for ninety years? You can't!" she screamed, her words dripping with venom and absolute loathing.

"I suppose I should thank you for setting him aflame," Jaqueline continued a bit more calmly, her dark eyes demonstrating absolutely no gratitude whatsoever. "But you got what *I* wanted. What *I* endured Lorenzo's torture for. And that can't be forgiven."

"What did I get?" Nora whispered, suspecting she knew the answer, but needing to hear Jaqueline say it aloud.

"Silence! I am still speaking. Don't you want to hear my story?" Jaqueline demanded, giving a smile that sent Nora's skin crawling. Now she wasn't entirely sure who the most unhinged and dangerous Vampire in the room was anymore—Rodriguez or Jaqueline.

Nora gave a small nod, not wanting to provoke anymore outbursts.

"Where was I? Oh yes, I betrayed Lorenzo by having Endre dug up. I can see by the look of surprise on your face you might actually be putting the pieces together by now. I'd suspected you were bright all along, otherwise, I didn't see how you could hold his interest," Jaqueline taunted with a glower.

"I recruited that one," Jaqueline continued, gesturing to Micelli's still body lying on the floor, "to do my dirty work. Fortunately it wasn't very hard. I'm very good at getting men to fall in love with me ... except the one I want, of course. I convinced Dave here that in order for us to be together, I needed to be human. I told him there was a way. A cure. But only one Vampire knew the formula and he was long buried. Dave, like a gentleman, offered to dig up the corpse I needed, but we needed to be more discreet lest Lorenzo catch wind of our plan. He did eventually, but by then Endre had already whisked you away to Paris. Dave arranged for your little expedition to come, hoping you would do just what you did and release Endre. He also arranged for the raid on your lab in Germany, and you know the rest."

"If you wanted the cure, why didn't you just ask us for it?" Nora puzzled, flabbergasted by all the cloak and dagger operations that had gone into something which could have been a simple request.

"I'm still talking you little cunt!" Jaqueline screamed.

Nora took a step back, slamming solidly into Rodriguez. Right now, she would probably take Rodriguez over Jaqueline. Maybe.

"It was never about the cure! I don't want a fucking cure! I wanted *him*. It was always about Endre. The plan was simple, he was going to come to Paris and rescue *me*. He was going to see *me* and realize how much he needed *me*, but you had to ruin it! You couldn't keep your legs closed, could you, you little slut? As soon as he fucked you, he forgot I even existed. Do you know how many times I made my feelings for him known? Do you know what he said? He said he still loved his *wife*. His *dead* wife. And he would never love another," Jaqueline raved. "He.

Lied," she whispered dangerously. "He will atone for his lies later." She glanced over at Endre's still-unconscious form.

"But this one," Jaqueline persisted, delivering a brutal kick to Micelli, "started to get out of hand. He started to have suspicions about my motives and my adoration of him, so he began keeping information from me. He'd known where you were all along, holed up in this lab. I think some poor, pathetic part of him still believed I was after the cure so I could be with him, and not just after your location so I could take your head and Endre's heart."

Rodriguez's arm squeezed tightly around Nora's throat in a gesture more possessive than threatening.

"You said I get to kill her," Rodriguez growled in a low voice.

"Yes, yes." Jaqueline waved her hand dismissively. "Let's not squabble about which one of us gets to kill her. We'll flip a coin for it later, or something, all right?"

Rodriguez growled low in his throat and Nora felt the vibrations through her back from his chest.

The sound of stirring drew Jaqueline's intense attention from Nora to where Endre lay on the floor. His head moved slightly and relief flooded Nora—at least he was still alive.

"Throw her in with the nurse, the humans should stick together," Jaqueline taunted with a laugh. "And take him out of here, too. I don't care what you do with him until the delivery," she said, gesturing vaguely to Jackson.

Nora felt Endre's gaze on her before she saw his eyes were open. She opened her mouth to warn him about Jaqueline, but Rodriguez slapped a hand across her lips to render her mute before she could get a word out.

"Get her out of here!" Jaqueline ordered before turning to Endre, an expression of sweet innocence masking the scorn she'd worn earlier.

As Rodriguez dragged Nora from the room, her eyes locked with Endre's, pleading for him to see Jaqueline for what she really was.

"Endre," Jaqueline crooned sweetly to him.

"It doesn't matter what she said," Rodriguez rumbled dangerously in her ear as he toted Nora down the hall. "You're mine. You have no idea the hell I went through because of you. I'll get my pound of flesh before this is over. We'll play again soon, sweetheart."

When he reached Jackson's bedroom, Rodriguez opened the door and shoved her inside. The door slammed behind her with a definitive clank and Nora wondered if she'd ever see Endre alive again with what Rodriguez had in store for her.

CHAPTER TWO

Watching Rodriguez drag Nora from the room, Endre realized he'd never known true terror until that moment. There was a very real possibility he may never see her again.

"Endre," a voice crooned from beside him, a voice he knew once a long time ago.

Managing to wrench his gaze from the empty doorway where Nora had been led away, Endre faced Jaqueline—the woman he had considered a sister from the moment he brought her into the world of blood and shadows. He had always looked after her as though she was his own flesh and blood, but observing her now, he wasn't sure if he'd ever really known her. There was a manic look in her eyes that had chased away the woman he had known so many years ago. But it *was* her. He'd know her anywhere.

"Jaqueline," he stated, not bothering to question the sight before him. "I thought you were dead." This time, he was unable to keep the surprise from his voice.

"No, my love," she answered softly, placing a gentle hand on his cheek. "You were misled. That bitch lied to you."

Endre growled at the slight to Nora. But *had* she lied to him? He could see no reason she would. She didn't even know who Jaqueline was when she'd seen Lorenzo's blood memory, so she would have had no idea what Jaqueline meant to Endre. All his instincts communicated to him Jaqueline was the one not to be trusted in all this. She was, after all, the only one unbound in this scenario.

"Nora told me Lorenzo had a gun to your head," Endre remarked, trying to remember what it was exactly Nora had divulged of the blood memory. He did remember she hadn't seen the outcome, not knowing if Jaqueline had died at Lorenzo's hands, but that it seemed fairly likely.

"He did, but he let me go," Jaqueline gloated with a triumphant smile. "He said he couldn't bear to kill something he loved so much. But I never loved him. I did what I had to do. I said what I had to in order to survive."

Endre knew what was coming. Over the years, she had hinted that her feelings for him went beyond the familial bond he'd felt. He'd always tried to deflect her advances gently so he wouldn't hurt her. He had thought she'd finally given up when she was with Gregor, but it appeared his hopes had been misguided.

"I loved you, Endre. I always did. You once told me you couldn't be with me because you were still in love with Ingrid. You told me you would never love another woman after her. You *lied,* Endre. But I'm willing to look past that. Now that I know you *can* love another woman, I'm giving you another chance." She smiled sweetly at him, but he could see the rage simmering beneath, given away by the slight tick in her lower right eyelid.

Endre weighed his options. Did he attempt to placate her, and take the chance she would know he was lying? Or should he tell her the truth: Nora was it for him? Both seemed like dangerous options if he was entirely honest with himself.

"What's it going to be?" Jaqueline prompted.

"Jaqueline," Endre started, "you are like a sister to me. I do love you, but clearly not in the way you desire. I truly am sorry, but I cannot reciprocate your feelings." He did his best to show her the sincerity in his words with the pained expression on his face.

"It's because of her, isn't it?" Jaqueline raged. "It's because you love her that you cannot love me? Well, no matter, your little human will be dead soon."

Human?

"Oh, you didn't know?" Jaqueline taunted with a laugh when she saw the confusion on his face. "Nora has been injected with the cure. I hope you worked out all the kinks. Now she's a fragile, helpless human. She was so frail and weak Rodriguez had to carry her from the room. Poor thing was barely able to stand on her own two feet. Between you and me, I don't think she'll last much longer." Jaqueline gave Endre an exaggerated look of sorrow and shook her head sadly. "Especially if Rodriguez gets to her first," she whispered in his ear.

Endre struggled against the chains binding him, intent on erasing her thinly veiled threat from the air around him. He couldn't bear the thought of Nora suffering at the hands of that lunatic again.

Taking a step back, Jacqueline appraised Endre's struggling form with a deep sigh.

"I knew you would never choose me over her. But I'm confident you will see my exemplary qualities once she's out of the picture," she said matter-of-factly. "Take him away," she ordered Rodriguez—who had returned without Nora in hand—Jaqueline's voice taking on a regal tone as if she thought herself royalty.

Rodriguez scowled first at Jaqueline, then down at Endre, but did as he was bidden and grasped onto the chains keeping Endre bound and helpless.

"Wait!" Jaqueline stomped over to them. "So you don't get yourself into any trouble," she explained and snapped his neck.

CHAPTER THREE

"Jody?" A soft voice, and an even softer touch, ran a hand over her back, and brought her up from the depths of her dream.

In truth, she was glad to be woken; there were only so many times someone could watch their sister die on a constant loop without losing all their marbles. Jody felt like she was already a few short after the last couple of days, and thought it might be best if she held tight to the rest of them.

Lifting her head from the pillow, Jody looked at the woman sitting beside her on the bed. She didn't remember laying down or falling asleep, only her anguish and pain and the tears blinding her vision. The tears were gone, her vision clear, but she still had no idea who the woman next to her was or how she knew her name.

"I'm Nora," the woman explained quietly, folding her hands together in her lap. "I was friends with Alicia."

Jody appraised Nora critically. Alicia had never spoken of a friend named Nora. But then again, Alicia had never told her anything about her run-in with

Micelli either. It was highly likely Alicia had made a few new friends in recent days.

"Are you a Vampire?" Jody whispered, taking in the pale color of Nora's skin and the larger-than-average pupils she'd assessed were common with Vampires.

"Not anymore," Nora choked out in a broken sob.

Jody was taken aback by the sudden outburst of emotion, unsure how to react.

Of course, her compassion won out in the end and she wrapped her arms around Nora, pulling her into a tight embrace. Jody didn't know if it was really very wise to hug a Vampire … or former-Vampire. The only ones she'd known were violent creatures until she met Zeke. She just hoped Nora was closer to the Zeke end of the spectrum than the Rodriguez end.

The two of them held one another for a few moments before Nora's shuddering sobs quieted, and Jody's tears had dried up. Jody doubted their captors would be too concerned with her hydration, so she attempted to quell her tears. It was difficult though. Sometimes the heart just needed to be heard even when the head knew it would only do her harm.

Drawing in a deep, shaky breath, Nora gave Jody one last squeeze before pulling away.

Giving Jody a dour smile, she apologized, "I'm sorry, sometimes you just need to get it out, you know?"

"I do know," Jody acknowledged, giving her a watery smile in return.

Standing from the bed, Nora paced the room for a few moments. Her steps were halted and unsteady, making Jody nervous she was going to fall. Nora stumbled and Jody jumped up to keep her from crashing to the floor.

"Here, I think you need to lie down," she offered, giving up her space on the bed.

Nora positioned herself on her side, and watched Jody as she took up the path Nora had abandoned. Her assessing eyes made Jody uneasy, but there was no malice in them. Maybe this woman *was* her sister's friend. She was, after all, locked in here with Jody and not running amok out there with Rodriguez and Micelli.

"How did you know Alicia?" Jody finally asked, unable to endure the silence of the room or Nora's watchful gaze. She hated she was referring to her sister in past tense. The thought almost brought on a new round of tears.

"I hadn't known her long, just the few days she'd been here," Nora confessed, tucking a hand under her cheek, making her appear young and innocent.

Jody got the impression Nora was a few years younger than her, but it was hard to tell. Especially for someone who had said she had been a Vampire.

"What was she doing here? And earlier you said you were no longer a Vampire. How can you stop being a Vampire?" Jody sputtered. There were still so many questions left unanswered, she hoped Nora could provide some insight.

"Those answers are pretty close to one and the same," Nora admitted with a wry smile. "Your sister was here working on a cure for Vampirism. She was brilliant, you know."

Jody nodded; she did know. Alicia had always been brilliant.

"She figured out in a few days what Endre had worked for decades on."

"Alicia came up with a cure?" Jody questioned, unable and not wanting to hide the amazement in her voice. "How is that possible? I just imagined Vampirism was irreversible to the body."

"She figured something out. I suppose we'll find out pretty quickly how well it worked," Nora proclaimed with a grimace.

"Meaning?" Jody inquired, looking Nora over warily.

"Meaning, I was injected with a dose of it … by Rodriguez. I was using the syringe as a weapon when they burst into the lab. That plan backfired. He injected me instead of me stabbing him."

"Did it work?" Jody asked, curiosity taking hold of her.

"We didn't know what the effects were yet, so I'm still not even sure how fast things are supposed to work."

"Do you feel any different?" Stopping her pacing, Jody moved toward where Nora lay on the bed.

"I still feel … hungry," Nora explained, "but it's different than it was before."

"What else?" Jody asked, crouching so her face was level with Nora's. She couldn't help it, her nurse's instincts took over.

Nora beckoned her closer, and Jody hesitated before leaning in.

"My senses still work the same," Nora whispered in her ear, then pulled back. "For now anyway. I didn't want them to hear," she clarified, gesturing to the world outside their little room.

Climbing to her feet, Jody continued pacing. There might be hope for an escape if Nora had retained some of her Vampire attributes. But they didn't know if that was a temporary phenomenon or if that was how Alicia designed the cure to work. Jody glanced over at Nora on the bed, she was fairly confident Nora's strength had waned considerably.

"I feel very weak, though," Nora declared, reading the doubt in Jody's eyes. "I don't know about the immortality piece, but I'd rather not test the theory," Nora confessed with a mirthless smile.

"Me either," Jody acknowledged as she continued her pacing.

"Shit," Nora swore under her breath, drawing Jody's attention back to the bed.

"What is it? Are you feeling worse?" Jody asked urgently.

"They just broke Endre's neck," Nora whispered, her round eyes hinting at the terror she felt.

"Oh God," Jody replied, her hand covering the sob threatening to escape.

"He's still alive," Nora reassured, though Jody was fairly certain the reassurance was for the both of them. "Or, at least he will be."

"That's insane," Jody couldn't help but whisper. "How do you kill a Vampire?" If she had any hope of doing *anything* against the invading Vampires, it might do her some good to know exactly how to kill one.

"Remove the head or stop the heart," Nora confided solemnly.

A vision of Alicia lying on the floor, bleeding from her chest forced its way into her brain.

"Alicia was shot in the chest," Jody whispered. "So, even if she had ingested Vampire blood, she couldn't come back, could she?" She hated herself for the hopeful note in her voice.

"Honestly, I don't know," Nora answered.

"So, it's a possibility?" Jody questioned excitedly.

Jody didn't particularly enjoy the thought of her sister coming back as a Vampire, but if what Nora said was true about there being a cure, at least there was some hope Alicia could live out a normal life—or at least a semi-normal life—if she were to come back.

"I'm sorry, Jody, but I wouldn't get my hopes up if I were you," Nora admitted gently. "I've never seen or heard of a transition taking this long to go into effect."

"You're saying if she hasn't woken up a Vampire yet, it's unlikely she will?"

Nora nodded in response.

Jody tried to think back to Zeke's blood memory of his transition and where he was when he awoke. He had already made it down to the morgue. Her brain calculated the amount of time that would have had to pass between when he died in the emergency room and being taken down to the lower level of the hospital. Surely more time had elapsed for Zeke before transition than had for Alicia. Jody clung to that tiny sliver of hope, but didn't share it with Nora. Nora was just trying to help and protect her in a way, but right now, Jody needed that shard of hope to keep her going.

CHAPTER FOUR

The last thing Nora wanted to do was dash Jody's hopes to pieces. She could remember a time when hope was the only thing keeping her from unraveling. But she also wanted to make sure she was realistic. Giving someone false hope could be just as detrimental as telling them a hard truth.

Closing her eyes, Nora tried to fight off the exhaustion weighing her down. Now was quite the inopportune time to be decrepit on a bed. Endre needed her, Jody needed her, and she suspected Jackson and Zeke were still in the building, too, and needed her. She may not be a Vampire anymore, but she could still hear like one and now seemed as good a time as any to test just how far her abilities had diminished … if at all.

Heartbeats sounded in Nora's head when she tuned out all the other noises around her. The closest and loudest belonged to Jody in the room with her. She counted two more in the hallway. Her mind wandered her mental map of the building, placing imaginary pushpins at the locations she heard others in the building. She had no idea who was where or how many of the heartbeats belonged to guards. She tried to listen for voices, but an eerie quiet settled over the facility. When her count reached ten, she heard nothing more.

"Nora, are you all right?" Jody's voice came from far off.

"Ten," Nora mumbled aloud.

"What?" Jody came closer in an attempt to understand her better.

"I hear ten heartbeats within the building, including yours and mine," Nora explained.

"Is Zeke here?" Jody questioned excitedly, and Nora knew immediately there was more to the pair than just a Vampire hired to rescue a damsel in distress.

"I can't tell whose is whose," Nora admitted sourly. "If someone was talking, I would be able to at least make out their voices, but it's unusually quiet out there."

"What can Micelli be doing?" Jody wondered aloud.

Nora cracked an eye and looked up at her. She'd forgotten Jody wasn't in the room when Micelli collapsed in the lab, and her hearing wasn't acute enough that she would have heard the guards in their feeble attempt to wrangle Jody into assisting.

"What is it?" Jody implored, her brow creased in either concern or confusion.

"Micelli's on the floor in the lab … or at least that's where Jaqueline left him before she had me removed."

"What happened to him?" Jody gasped. "Is he dead?" There was a hint of glee in her voice, and Nora couldn't say she blamed her one bit.

"I don't think he's dead, but he's unconscious," Nora acknowledged. "I don't know what she's going to do with him. He collapsed shortly after you were taken from the room. She wouldn't let anyone help him. The guards were going to bring you back in, but she stopped them."

"Jackie did? Why?" Jody queried, aghast.

Clearly Jody also didn't know who Jackie really was.

"Jackie isn't who you think she is," Nora pointed out.

"And who do I think she is?" Jody was watching Nora in a way that was unnerving, like she thought Nora might require a straitjacket or similar restraint.

"I assume you think she is your sister's friend and co-worker?" Nora pressed, her eyebrows raised to keep her eyes from falling closed of their own accord.

"If that's not who she is, then how does she figure into all this?" Jody questioned, her frustration clear. "I think I've had enough mystery in the previous week to last me a few decades."

"She's a Vampire. Apparently she orchestrated this whole thing. She was behind exhuming Endre's body, the attack on our lab in Germany, and now the kidnapping of both you and your sister," Nora told her, still a bit shocked herself at those revelations. Jaqueline was essentially the Moriarty to Endre's Sherlock.

"Wait, Endre's body being exhumed? Lab in Germany? I have no idea what you're talking about," Jody confessed, shaking her head.

Nora chuckled to herself. The story of the last several months of her life seemed like some horrific plotline from a sick and twisted movie, she had almost forgotten it wasn't a well-known tale. Nora regaled the saga that was her life as of late, and nearly giggled at the ridiculous faces Jody made with each additional obstacle or tragedy that had befallen her.

"Wow. Just, wow," Jody remarked, shaking her head when Nora finished. "I can't believe that all really happened."

"It happened." Nora closed her eyes again. She was exhausted, and reliving all her misadventures had taken a toll on the remnants of energy she clung to.

"You need to rest," Jody urged, laying her hand on Nora's hair.

Nora didn't know if it was her presence as a caregiver, or if it was something else, but Jody's touch on her calmed her and she drifted off to sleep.

CHAPTER FIVE

Endre returned to the land of the living with a gasp followed by a low groan. Rolling his neck from side to side, he stretched it, making sure his vertebrae had healed back into place properly. He'd only experienced his neck snapping a handful of times over his thousand plus years, but it was a rough emergence each and every time. With a stab wound, or even a gunshot wound, his body would push out any foreign objects and seal itself closed; it was a quick process with minimal pain. Having his neck broken meant the mending of major nerve pathways. The intricacies took time, and could only be completed once the bones making up his spine had been pulled back into place by connective tissues.

"Welcome back," Jaqueline's voice greeted him before he'd even had a chance to open his eyes.

Her voice grated against those newly repaired nerves in a way it never had before. Endre wondered if this derangement had always been present and he never noticed it before, or if it had developed over the time Lorenzo held her as his captive. From his own imprisonment within his grave, he knew the mind could quickly unravel when it had difficulty grasping the situation the body was in. He wanted to believe this was not the woman he'd considered a sister and treated as such. He desired to believe Lorenzo was to blame for the insanity the lilt in her voice betrayed. It seemed unfathomable she had always been like this and he hadn't noticed.

"Endre?" Jaqueline called after him as he strolled through his sprawling gardens.

Turning, he found her rushing behind him, her skirts held aloft so they didn't drag along the stone pathway. Seeing Jaqueline in his sanctuary was not a rarity in itself, but at this hour it was unprecedented.

"Jaqueline, what are you doing here? You need to go home to Gregor before the sun rises," he chided, smiling kindly down at the woman he thought of as a sister.

"Something bad is happening, you need to leave," she warned.

"What has happened?" Endre asked, escorting the frantic woman to a table situated under a large tree.

"You must listen to me, you need to leave here," she pleaded, her eyes round with terror.

"Jaqueline, tell me what has happened," he demanded, his voice growing stern. He didn't have the patience to deal with a woman's hysterics, even Jaqueline's.

"I think he means to kill you," she whispered, voice full of dread.

"Who, Jaqueline, who?" Endre implored. It took everything in his power not to shake the answer from her.

"Lorenzo," Jaqueline answered.

"Lorenzo is one of my closest friends," Endre warned. He may love Jaqueline, but he'd known Lorenzo far longer. "I think it would be best if you left now. Go home before dawn."

"Endre," she pleaded, grasping onto his shirt. "Please, you have to listen to me. I cannot lose you. I love you."

Endre softened, but only slightly. "Go home to Gregor." When she opened her mouth to protest once again, he held up a hand to silence her. "Go."

It wasn't more than ten minutes later Lorenzo had arrived and passed judgement on Endre for the crime he himself committed. How wrong he'd been about his friend. How wrong he'd been about Jaqueline.

"Endre, are you even listening to me?" Jaqueline demanded.

His eyes remained closed while Endre was stuck in the memory of their encounter in his garden. That spark of insanity hadn't been there, he was sure of it. But there was something there he'd misinterpreted for so long. He'd always thought her love for him was familial, like one would love a brother, just as he loved her as a sister. If he paid enough attention to the memory, he could see clearly now what he had been so blind to then.

"You never really did listen to me," she continued, her breath warm against his face.

If he opened his eyes now, he would find her dark eyes boring into him—eyes no longer resembling those of his Jaqueline from nearly a century ago.

"Even when I warned you!" she screamed, a spray of spittle landing on his cheek. "Look at me! For once if your fucking life, *actually look at me!*"

Endre complied to appease her; she deserved that much from him after how he'd brushed aside her affection for so many years, even if he didn't realize what it meant. His blue eyes met her dark ones, almost too close to his to focus on the individual flecks of color in the narrow ring of her irises. They were a deep chocolate brown to match the hue of her hair, a testament to her Mediterranean roots. She was a beautiful woman, or had been before the manic light took over her eyes and twisted her mouth into a permanent scowl. He remembered when she used to smile and how it lit up her entire face.

"What do you see when you look at me?" she inquired quietly, her eyes darting between his.

"I see a broken woman," Endre answered as honestly as he could. "He destroyed you, didn't he?"

"You destroyed me long before Lorenzo ever laid hands on me."

Taking several steps back, Jaqueline glared at him with hands on shapely hips. Endre could see how both the likes of Lorenzo and Micelli had fallen for her charms. But when he looked at her, he felt no stirring in his heart, no warming of his loins, no singing of his soul. Those reactions were reserved for Nora and Nora alone. Endre had never felt the things he felt with Nora even with his late wife, Ingrid.

"Do you know what it did to me, knowing I had come to you with my concerns for your safety and you merely brushed them aside? So often, I would relive the memory of your burial in my darkest hours. Even after you cast me aside, I still wondered what more I could have done to spare you your fate. I dreamed you lay in your grave, longing for me, like a stupid, love-sick little girl.

"Even after you were freed, which was *my* doing, I still held onto hope you would see me as I see you. But then you gave *her* what I pined centuries for!" Jaqueline raved.

"I never promised you anything. In either words or actions."

"Oh, I know that now," she admitted with a devilish smile. "I've been watching the two of you for a while. I can see the way you look at each other. You never looked at me the way you do her. Not once. So much love. So much *fear*. You fear she won't love you with the same intensity you love her. You fear for her safety. You fear her *death*," Jaqueline pressed. Her elongation of the last word held more than warning, it held promise.

Indeed, fear crept up Endre's spine. He'd been a warrior in the Viking age when he'd first transitioned into a Vampire. He'd fought countless battles, and never once did he feel the same icy dread as he did when he thought about losing Nora.

Jaqueline circled closer to him, around the back of the upright table where he was restrained, trailing a finger along the cold metal. When she came to stand in front of him again, she smiled, though it held no warmth.

"How does it feel?" She leaned close so her lips nearly touched his, and he felt the warm puffs of air across his mouth with each spoken word. "To fear for the life of the one you love?"

Endre understood now. He'd thought she was still trying to win his affection, but he had once again mistaken her intentions. She didn't want his love, not anymore. Jaqueline only wanted revenge for the perceived wrongs she felt he'd done her. And she intended to dole out that revenge using Nora.

CHAPTER SIX

Holding his breath, Endre waited for Jaqueline to make her next move. Her threats had extended to Nora, but he still had no idea what was in store for him. He didn't suspect she would stop at destroying his heart, she would want to tear apart his body, too. If any of the old Jaqueline he'd know still maintained residence in the Vampire he saw before him, she wouldn't do things by halves. She never had.

"I can see questions written across your face, Endre," Jaqueline taunted, "What happened to that stoic façade you used to wear which gave nothing of your thoughts away?"

Where, indeed. The last thing Endre needed right now was Jaqueline having a direct link to his thoughts. She already knew where to hit to hurt him the most, he didn't want her gleaning anything else from him.

"I wonder which would hurt more," Jaqueline pondered, looking up at the ceiling and tapping her chin thoughtfully. She paced in front of him for a beat before pursing her lips and continuing to voice her train of thought, "Would it hurt you more if I had Rodriguez go fetch Nora and she watched while he pummeled your face into something far less handsome? Or, if I sent Rodriguez to hurt Nora where you can only hear her and not see her? You would not be able to offer her any words of encouragement or comfort. But then again, you wouldn't be able to see the suffering either."

Jaqueline popped her lips in a gesture of thought before stopping in front of him.

"I can't decide which I like more. Maybe we'll do both. We'll have to have Rodriguez work you over first, because I don't know that Nora's frail human body would be able to take a beating from him," Jaqueline determined, giving him a face that twisted her features into some grotesque visage of a mock pout.

"You're not even going to deliver the pain yourself?" Endre taunted.

"Trying to get a rise out of me?" She laughed. "Oh, darling, you should know by now I don't get my hands dirty. That's what minions are for."

"I doubt he likes you referring to him as your minion," Endre admonished loudly, hoping to spark some kind of unrest between Jaqueline and Rodriguez. He'd already felt tension between them, all it would take would be one well-placed push to snap their fragile alliance.

"He's only here because of me. I pulled him from the wreckage of your little act of arson," Jaqueline stated.

"I thought you didn't get your hands dirty?" Endre challenged.

"I don't. And I didn't. I meant *I*, as in my resources. He owes me his second life, and he's obedient enough to recognize that," Jaqueline stated with arrogance.

"In time, you might find your confidence in his loyalty to you overstated," Endre warned.

"Just because you slew your master doesn't mean he's going to do the same to me," Jaqueline tittered.

"But you would do the same to *me*," Endre pointed out. "Do I not deserve the same loyalty you expect him to show, after having given you a second life?"

Jaqueline let out a hearty laugh that brought tears to her eyes. "Oh, Endre, and I always thought you lacked a sense of humor," she tittered, wiping at the corners of her eyes. "I owe you nothing, least of all my loyalty. You squandered it when you had that and more. Enough talk, I'm bored of it. I think I'm ready for a little entertainment."

The smile turning up the corners of her mouth was frightening.

"Minion," she called in a sing-song voice.

Rodriguez strode slowly into the room, and Endre could see the obvious clench of his jaw and the tick in the muscles. There was definitely unrest among Jaqueline's minions, Endre just needed to find a way to exploit it.

"Bring me that little bitch Nora," she spat.

Rodriguez looked up to meet Endre's gaze, and the glint of malice there rivaled what he saw when he looked into Jaqueline's eyes.

CHAPTER SEVEN

Jody paced the room after trying the lock on the door for the eighteen-hundredth time. She had no idea why she thought it might have miraculously unlocked itself, but it gave her something to do. She'd already examined the hinges on the door, but they weren't like the ones on her doors at home where all you needed was a screwdriver and something to hit it with to pop the pin out. Not that she had a screwdriver either. She'd also made a thorough inspection of the windows, and they were not the kind she could open … at all. She contemplated trying to break it, but figured she was more likely to hurt herself in the process and raise an alarm with all the noise than she was to break the damned thing. There was also the matter of Nora, who was too weak to make her own getaway, so Jody would have to find a way to get her out, too.

Opening her eyes, Nora turned her head slightly so Jody could see her face. Jody had been checking her breathing every few minutes, just to make sure she *was* breathing. Jody had no idea what was happening to her body with the injection of the cure, so she didn't know how to help her.

"What can I get you?" Jody offered, kneeling next to the bed.

"I don't know." Nora had answered the same way each of the other times Jody had asked the question.

"I'm sorry, I'm just going stir crazy," Jody apologized, getting to her feet again. "I don't like watching you suffer and not knowing what to do to help."

"I don't even know what I need," Nora explained. Again. Jody suspected she was getting a teensy bit annoyed with her incessant requests to assist in some way.

Nora sucked in a sharp breath and Jody had to fight to urge to ask again what she could do to help. Instead, she watched Nora's head turn toward the door.

"He's coming," she whispered. Jody didn't have to ask who. The look of trepidation on Nora's face told her everything she needed to know.

Loud crashing from outside their makeshift prison cell startled them both, making Jody jump.

"What was that?" she asked, hoping Nora's advanced sense of hearing could give them a clue as to what the hell was going on beyond the walls.

The noise came again, and this time with it shouting.

Directing her gaze at Jody, Nora whispered, "They're coming for you now. Something's happened in the lab."

"Is it Alicia?" Jody questioned, her voice hopeful.

"I don't know, I can't tell. There's so much going on, I can't separate everything out," Nora explained, shaking her head slightly.

The door to their prison flew open suddenly, smacking into the wall and creating a divot in the drywall where the handle hit. Standing as gigantic and imposing as the first time she'd laid eyes on him was Rodriguez. Without a word, he grabbed onto Jody's arm and dragged her toward the door.

"What's happening? Is it my sister?" she inquired, knowing better than to resist the tugging at her arm. She didn't feel adding broken bones to her list of concerns was a good move right now.

"Shut up," Rodriguez ordered. He pulled her through the door, and just before he closed it, he glanced over at Nora. "Don't worry, sweetheart, I'll be back for you later."

Rodriguez dragged Jody down the hall at a pace she had a hard time keeping up with. She vaguely knew the way to the lab from the room they were being held in, but the sharp turns he took around the corners sent her careening into walls and smacking into his hard frame. When they rounded the final corner and came to the doorway, the scene before her sent her stomach roiling.

Jody stood with her mouth agape as she tried to make sense of the lab. Alicia's body lay still on the floor, just as she left it hours earlier. Next to it, however, was a new body. Without a head. Jody's eyes traced the trail of blood from the fresh corpse to the severed head, and she brought her hand to her mouth in an attempt to keep the meager contents of her stomach intact.

"Figure out what's wrong with him!" Rodriguez shouted as he shoved her farther into the room.

Jody stumbled, her eyes still glued to the new body. She was confused for a moment, thinking he referred to the headless man on the floor. She peered up into Rodriguez's furious face in confusion, only to see his gaze was neither directed at the decapitated body, nor at her. Turning, Jody was shocked to see Micelli being restrained—barely—by two of the Vampire guards. His eyes were a ghastly, solid black covering even where the whites should be. He snapped his jaws at his captors, but Jody didn't see any fangs. Foam oozed from the corners of his mouth, giving him the countenance of a rabid beast. He didn't look like a Vampire, but she had no idea *what* he was.

"What's wrong with him?" one of the guards shouted at her while continuing to attempt to restrain Micelli.

Another well-placed shove between her shoulder blades from Rodriguez brought Jody within feet of the writhing beast. Micelli's attention turned toward her and an animalistic growl sounded from deep in his chest. Jody scrambled backward, only to slip on the blood still slicking the floor and collide with Rodriguez again. His unyielding grip squeezed her shoulders, and for a second, just a second, she was glad he was behind her. After that second and her temporary insanity wore off, she remembered he hated her and it was highly unlikely he would do a thing to protect her from Micelli when he broke loose from the other two guards' grappling hands. Jody was fairly certain by the way they struggled to contain him, that was going to be sooner rather than later.

"Get over there," Rodriguez ordered through gritted teeth.

Guiding her by the shoulders, Rodriguez placed Jody so she stood even closer to Micelli than before. She got the vague impression of a virgin being led to the sacrifice … except for the virgin part.

She stood precisely where Rodriguez planted her. There was no way she was getting any closer to those snapping teeth. Even without Vampire fangs, those things were dangerous. She wasn't going to lose a hand just so she could check his pulse. Jody had no idea what they expected her to do for him. This was unlike any malady she'd ever encountered. None of the symptoms made sense to her, and frankly, his eyes freaked her the fuck out. They were unnatural. She'd *never* seen that happen before. She was pretty sure she'd never even *heard* of that happening before.

"Quit fucking staring at him, and *do* something!" Rodriguez roared behind her, his wrath competing with Micelli's wild condition for which was going to make her lose her shit first.

"I don't know what you expect me to do?" she pleaded, trying to turn to look at him, but his hands on her shoulders held her firm. "Do you have any idea what triggered this?"

Rodriguez's grip tightened. "Yeah, your fucking bitch sister injected him with the cure before we put a bullet in her."

"I don't know anything about the cure," Jody argued, her eyes glued to the blackness of Micelli's.

"I've heard that one before," Rodriguez snapped.

"I mean, I don't know the chemical makeup of it! I don't know what he's reacting to," she explained, shaking her head. "I don't know how to help him, I've never seen anything like this before."

"Well, you better think of something fast," Rodriguez threatened.

"Shoot him," a woman's voice came from the doorway.

Jackie strode into the room and stood glaring at Micelli, an expression of utter disgust twisting her otherwise beautiful face.

"He acts like a rabid dog, we put him down like a rabid dog. There's no coming back from this," she said dismissively and walked toward the door.

Jody watched the woman she thought was her sister's friend step over Alicia's body on her way to the exit. Another growl ripped from Micelli's chest and Jody heard the answering click of a bullet being loaded into the chamber of a gun. At least that's what she thought it sounded like; she had no experience with guns. A moment later she realized it was Rodriguez who held the gun, when his hand came over her shoulder holding it. He was going to shoot Micelli point blank, with her directly in front of him, *and* give her hearing damage. She tried to take a step back, but was impeded by Rodriguez's solid chest.

Real panic set in then. She may deal with gunshot victims at the hospital and dead bodies from time to time, but she'd never gotten up close and personal with the process. She didn't want to start now. Jody turned in Rodriguez's iron grip and did the most ridiculous thing she could have—buried her face in his chest.

CHAPTER EIGHT

A gunshot echoed throughout the room, and it was deafening. Jody vaguely remembered letting out a scream and covering her ears with her hands, her face still pressed to Rodriguez. But the shot didn't silence the snarls and wild noises from Micelli, and Jody didn't even want to know how he survived the shot to the forehead Rodriguez had been aiming for. In fact, the chaos around her grew louder through the minimalistic muffling her hands provided.

"Get him!" Rodriguez's voice shouted into Jody's ear.

Another shot went off and she screamed again at the eardrum-bursting report. A cacophony of metallic crashing erupted around her, accompanied by more shouting. Jody wanted to open her eyes to see what was happening, she really did, but couldn't find the courage to.

"Stop fucking crying," Rodriguez chastised, and she knew the order was for her when she became aware of the wetness on her cheeks.

Her body was wrenched away from the solidarity of his chest, and her eyes flew open when she hurtled toward the ground. Jody tried to twist so she didn't land on her wrist, and took the brunt of the impact with her hip instead. It hurt like a mother, but at least it was less likely she'd sustain a sprain or a break. On impact, her body slid a foot across the floor flooded with the blood of two victims, until she landed against the feet of a workbench.

Shouts continued to sound through the room, echoing off the white tiled walls. Jody watched the guards wrestle Micelli to the floor amidst the destruction his struggle had caused. Blood from the floor smeared across his face when they forced his head down. He looked like a beast that had clawed its way from the depths of hell, and he was in fine company with the rest of the inhabitants of the building. An unnerving smile spread across Micelli's face as he stared at her with those black eyes. A sense of foreboding tightened Jody's stomach and she scrambled under the table.

With a roar, Micelli rose to his feet, taking both Vampire guards—who should have easily been able to overpower him—with him. Another round of bullets passed through the air, none of them hitting their intended target, but one of them catching a guard in the chest. The guard dropped to the floor with a thud and the other was easily thrown off by Micelli, landing with a crash amongst the pile of twisted metal that had once been a table.

Rodriguez rushed toward the unfettered Micelli, and as a result was thrown into the wall next to the guard. Micelli turned and gave Jody a smirk before he ran from the room. It took Jody a few seconds of convincing herself that had really happened.

A grunt sounded from the direction the guard and Rodriguez had landed, and Jody crawled back farther under the workbench with nowhere to go. The only exit from the room was the one Micelli had just charged through, and to get to that, Jody would somehow have to move faster than two Vampires and get through the obstacle course containing destroyed lab equipment and a rising body count.

"Get after him," Rodriguez ordered, pointing the remaining guard in the direction Micelli had run.

"He's fled the building, he's no longer our concern. I couldn't care any less about what he does to the city. Fucking frozen wasteland. I don't know how people live in this goddamned tundra," Jackie's voice sounded from the lab doorway. "I gave you one job, and you couldn't even do that right," she chided Rodriguez.

Jackie's gaze swept across the room and landed on Jody under the workbench. It was cold and unsympathetic as she appraised Jody's cowering form.

"Grab her," Jackie ordered, nodding toward where Jody hid—not very well.

Jody didn't have time to move in any direction before she was in Rodriguez's grip again. She expected him to topple the workbench to get her out, but instead, he pulled her from her hiding place with uncharacteristic gentleness. His gentleness was more unnerving to Jody than his rough handling.

Rodriguez stood Jody before Jackie, just as he had done when she faced Micelli. Jackie looked her over with cold indifference. She seemed to weigh something before making a decision with a slow nod of her head.

"Shoot her," Jackie tossed out the order. "I don't think we need her for anything else. She was useless with Micelli, I see no reason to keep her around."

A gasp escaped from Jody. *Who the hell is this woman?*

"Jackie, please," Jody pleaded, not above begging for her life at this point, not when death was staring her straight in the face.

"Jackie?" Jackie laughed heartily. "No, dear, it's not Jackie. *Jaqueline.*"

"Jaqueline, please," Jody tried again, hoping the use and proper pronunciation of *Jaqueline's* name might appeal to some sense of mercy.

"If you can give me one reason to keep you alive, and I agree, I'll spare you," Jaqueline offered, an amused smirk gracing her lips.

"You were my sister's friend—" Jody started, but Jaqueline put up a hand and closed her eyes.

She shook her head slightly before replying. "If that is the argument you are going to use, you will not succeed. Do not try to appeal to my sense of emotion. I was never friends with your sister. Much like Micelli, she was a means to an end," Jaqueline confessed, looking down dispassionately at Alicia's body where she still lay on the floor.

"I'll do anything you want," Jody blurted out. Yeah, she wasn't above using the clichéd tactics of those who had been threatened with death who came before her. She had no shame. There was no shame in wanting to live.

"Anything?" Jaqueline asked, eyebrows raised. "That's so sweet. I don't think there's anything you could do for me to be worth the hassle of guarding you."

"How about anything *I* want?" Rodriguez's voice came from behind her.

A chill ran through Jody when she thought of the kinds of things Rodriguez would want from her. Was she prepared for that? *Anything to stay alive,* she told herself.

"Anything," she whispered with as much conviction as her wavering voice would allow.

"Well, I'll leave you two alone then," Jaqueline announced in a bored tone. She rolled her eyes and shook her head slightly before turning away. "Oh, clean up this mess, would you, minion? Or, better yet, have her do it," she tossed over her shoulder casually as she walked through the doorway.

When Jaqueline disappeared from the doorway, Rodriguez's grip loosened and the heat from him at the back of her body disappeared. Jody stood still, barely daring to breathe. What did he have in store for her?

"Oh, minion?" Jaqueline said, appearing in the doorway again. "You'll have to put your toy away for now. I need to feed. We're down a guard," her gaze tracked from one dead guard to the other, "or two. I need you to come with me."

Rodriguez's fist wrapped in Jody's hair and she let out a surprised screech. He'd been a few steps behind her, but moved so much faster than she could even comprehend.

"Take her," he offered, using her hair to tilt her head back.

Jody brought her hands up to where Rodriguez gripped her hair, trying to loosen his hold. Tears leaked from the corners of her eyes with each tiny tug.

Jaqueline curled her lips up in disgust when she looked at Jody. "I prefer the male variety," Jaqueline replied haughtily. "You're not getting out of this. I'm sorry you have to delay playtime, but your toy will be right where you left it when we get back." Her tone was just this side of condescending.

Frankly, Jody was surprised Rodriguez allowed Jaqueline to talk to him that way. From what Jody had seen of him, he didn't follow anyone's rules, so she didn't understand why he'd follow Jaqueline's.

"Oh, poor thing, she looks so confused," Jaqueline tittered. "I bet she's wondering how I keep such a big, bad dog like you on a leash. Well, sweetie, I can tell you right now, it's not by giving him *anything* he wants. He's never had a taste of my pussy, and he never will," she added, looking him up and down with the same disgusted look one might use when eyeing a nest of cockroaches.

"I suppose you're saving that dusty cooch for the bloodsucker in the other room who wants nothing to do with it," Rodriguez taunted with a laugh.

Jaqueline stiffened at his response and the condescending smile slid from her face, replaced with a look of fury. Her eyes flashed with the threat of violence, but somehow Jody didn't think Rodriguez felt intimidated.

"We'll play later," Rodriguez whispered in Jody's ear. "I've got to take the mistress out to dinner." While he spoke, his eyes never left Jaqueline.

Jaqueline spun on her heel and stomped from the room, leaving Jody alone with Rodriguez once more. His grip on her hair tightened, and he pulled her head back so it rested against his chest, her neck exposed to him. She took a deep breath and waited. She couldn't believe he hadn't already bitten her; he'd definitely shown more restraint than she'd ever given him credit for. His warm, wet tongue slithered from where her shoulder met her neck up to her ear, and she had to swallow to keep bile from rising in her throat. He unwound his hand from her hair and clasped it around her throat. Jody dropped her arms is resignation, bracing herself for pain. Burying his face in her loose hair, he inhaled deeply, letting out the breath with a moaning sigh. Had Zeke pulled that move on her, she would have been so wet. When Rodriguez did it, she wanted to crawl out of her skin. Tears pricked her eyes. She hoped Zeke was all right.

"Let's go! You'll get to feed soon enough!" Jaqueline's screech punched through the thick anticipation around Jody.

"She gets hangry," Rodriguez explained amidst Jaqueline's huffing and stomping footsteps.

It reminded Jody distinctly of a child throwing a tantrum when they didn't get their way. Rodriguez nipped at Jody's throat and she let out a whimper when his fang broke the skin. That *hurt*, and she knew it was only going to get worse.

"Now!" screamed Jaqueline from several rooms away.

Rodriguez chuckled before grabbing Jody roughly and marching her back to the room she shared with Nora. She'd dodged a bullet, miraculously thanks to Jaqueline, but she didn't think she'd be so lucky the next time around.

"Until we meet again," Rodriguez promised with a little bow when he brought her to the door. "I do so love the anticipation," he added, the glint in his eye terrifying all speech from Jody's brain.

The door clanged shut behind him, and she turned to face Nora, mouth agape.

"What the hell was that?" Nora questioned weakly.

"I have no idea," Jody answered honestly, sinking to the bed beside Nora to relieve her shaking legs. Unspent adrenaline was a bitch.

CHAPTER NINE

"Your dog not quite behaving as you planned?" Endre taunted while Jaqueline paced before him, presumably waiting for Rodriguez to finish up with Alicia's sister.

"Shut the fuck up," Jaqueline snapped, whirling to face him. Her eyes narrowed as she took in his gloating smile.

Rodriguez sauntered unhurriedly into the room, and Jaqueline's intense scrutiny shifted from Endre. Endre glanced at Rodriguez, too. Just the sight of him made his blood boil. He'd taken pains to seek out the worst of Nora's blood memories involving this particular fiend so he would better understand her trauma. It had taken her months to regain the fire of her former self, and Endre blamed the Vampire before him for that transformation. He supposed Jaqueline was indirectly responsible for Nora's suffering as well. In the end, however, it didn't matter if their hand in the pain caused to his beloved was direct or indirect … once he was free of these bindings, he would see to it they would both pay for their transgressions with their lives.

"What took you so long?" Jaqueline hissed at Rodriguez, the venomous look she had been giving to Endre earlier now focused on him. "When I tell you to do something, I mean *immediately,* not whenever the fuck you feel like it."

A smirk pulled at the corners of Rodriguez's lips and the rage coming off Jaqueline was palpable. Her body practically vibrated with fury, and Endre could see red creep across the skin of her neck. Rodriguez hadn't even had to respond with words to draw her ire. He had it now in full force.

"Let's go, grab the doctor, we'll drop him off on our way," Jaqueline ordered through gritted teeth.

Rodriguez grunted his acknowledgement of the order and left the room, but not before looking Endre over with a sneer. Endre responded with a scowl of his own.

"Where are you taking Jackson?" Endre ventured to ask Jaqueline before she exited the room.

Stopping, she stood still for a moment before turning slowly to face him. The corners of her mouth turned up into a Cheshire cat smile.

"You think you're so clever, don't you?" She let out a throaty laugh. "Since I am touched by your concern for your friend, I'll just tell you he has *other* friends who are very eager to be reunited with him."

Jaqueline continued to chuckle all the way out the door and down the hallway.

"Keep a close eye on that one," Jaqueline ordered one of the remaining guards. "You have my permission to break his neck if he gets out of hand."

Endre listened for the retreat of Jaqueline and Rodriguez through the building, Jackson with them. The roar of an engine outside confirmed their departure.

"Nora!" Endre yelled into the stillness of the room.

He had no idea where she was being kept, or if she would be able to hear him. If she'd still been a Vampire, he knew she would hear him. He hoped his call was loud enough in the otherwise empty building to carry to her location.

"Shut up in there!" the guard from down the hall answered instead.

"Endre!" a voice Endre didn't recognize answered a moment later. "Nora's here with me! She's weak."

Endre's stomach dropped. *She's weak.* Nora was weak. It was just as Jaqueline had said. Nora had been injected with the cure, and now her body was weakening.

"Please help her any way you can," Endre replied back, assuming the voice belonged to Alicia's sister.

"I said shut the fuck up!" the guard commanded, now standing in the doorway.

"Is Zeke in there with you?" Alicia's sister's voice came again, shaky this time.

Why can't I remember her name?

"No, he's not," Endre answered. He didn't know what Zeke looked like, but unless he was a guard in Jaqueline's employ, he wasn't here.

The guard strode angrily into the room, his jaw set and his fists clenched. His feet didn't even stop his advance before he threw his whole body into an impressive right hook to Endre's jaw. Endre groaned in pain, knowing damned well the bone was broken.

"That ought to keep you quiet for a while," the guard chuckled to himself, turning on his heel and resuming his post down the hall.

"Endre?" the sister's voice called again, her tone laced with panic.

The guard had only been half right. A broken jaw would keep him from speaking, but that didn't necessarily mean it would keep him quiet. Endre tapped out a message in Morse code, telling Nora to keep calm and of his love for her.

"What's happening?" Jody asked Nora anxiously.

Nora wished Jody would sit down and stop moving. She'd already had to close her eyes because the constant movement of Jody's pacing was making her dizzy. In truth, she had no idea what was happening, she just had little snippets of the conversation carried from the room Endre was being held in and what she had heard from Endre himself … which wasn't much. But at least she knew he was alive and he knew the same of her.

"He's not talking anymore, I think he's hurt," Nora relayed through the croak in her voice.

"Hurt?" Jody questioned, stopping her infernal pacing for a moment to stare at Nora.

"I think he got hit. Wherever it was, he isn't speaking anymore. I think he's trying to tap out Morse code though," Nora guessed, shaking her head. She sure wished she knew how to decipher it. "Do you know Morse code?"

Jody shook her head and her shoulders slumped. She looked more defeated than Nora had seen her since this whole ordeal became their reality.

"What do we do?" she queried, hugging her arms around her body.

Nora had no words of comfort or encouragement. She had no idea what to do.

"I can't just give up," Jody countered Nora's unspoken surrender, a determined expression on her face.

"Whatever you come up with, keep it quiet, they can hear you," Nora whispered, reminding Jody their guards were Vampires and could hear even their whispered conversations.

Dropping her head in her hands, Jody continued her incessant pacing. Now really would be the most opportune time to try to make an escape. From what Jody had told her, they were down two guards thanks to Micelli, and Jaqueline and Rodriguez were out of the building. Nora could account for six heartbeats nearby. They already knew Jackson had been taken from the building but they still didn't know where Zeke was. That meant there were either two or three Vampire guards patrolling the building. It would be sufficient personnel to keep two humans and one incapacitated Vampire in check.

Jody suddenly stopped pacing and turned to Nora, her eyes shining with hope again. "What if we—"

Shaking her head, Nora pressed a finger to her lips in the universal sign for silence.

"Oh, yeah," Jody whispered, "I forgot."

Nora slid over on the bed when Jody hurried over, giving hand gestures and mouthing words she couldn't even begin to decode. Nora shrugged her shoulders and Jody hung her head in defeat. It was like watching a silent film where everything is overacted to relay a message, except here, Nora couldn't tell what the hell that message was.

Perking up, Jody suddenly sprang up from the bed. She rummaged through drawers and piles of debris in the room, searching for only Jody knew what. Emerging from the depths of a drawer, she gave a triumphant wave of her hands ... in which she clutched a small notepad and a pen.

Pen and paper would certainly work a lot better to convey whatever plan Jody concocted than the mime routine she'd tried out earlier. Jody settled back onto the bed next to Nora, and they both stared down at the paper as Jody's hands scrawled across the page, outlining a plan for escape.

CHAPTER TEN

Cold air rushing over his skin awoke Jackson. The slight ache in his neck reminded him it'd been his vertebrae snapping that sent him into his latest bout of unconsciousness. It didn't, however, reveal any clues as to how long he'd been out or where he was now. The swaying movement and engine sounds gave him some pretty good ideas, though. He was definitely in a vehicle, and—judging by the frigid temperatures and the wind—the back of a truck. Jackson would even bet it was *his* truck. He didn't doubt that asshole Micelli was above using Jackson's own vehicle to carry out whatever sinister plans were afoot.

Jackson couldn't see a damned thing. It had been months since he had experienced total darkness. Reaching a hand toward his face, he found they were bound together. He should have expected that—if they were going to blindfold him, they were most definitely going to bind his hands. The driver of the truck took a sharp turn and Jackson threw his hands out in front of him to steady his slide across the bed. Metal clanked across the bed liner and Jackson swore under his breath as chain links dug into his skin.

"He's awake," a muffled female voice from inside the cab of the truck announced.

"We're almost there. We'll drop him off and then you can hunt," a voice Jackson knew well responded.

Rodriguez.

The truck took another turn and Jackson stuck his feet out to keep from sliding the other way across the bed. It was evident Rodriguez was deliberately taking the turns like a maniac so Jackson would smash against the sides of the truck. The constant movement and the need to brace against something robbed Jackson of the opportunity to inspect his bonds and find a way out of them.

True to Rodriguez's word, a few minutes later the truck drew to a halt.

"Stay here, this will only take a minute," Rodriguez ordered the woman in the truck. "Trust me, you don't want to go in there."

"Just hurry the fuck up," the woman barked, the demand a far cry from her earlier tone.

Rodriguez's only response was the slamming of the truck door hard enough to shake the whole vehicle. Rough hands grabbed Jackson and he kicked toward the direction they came from, but his feet connected only with air. A low growl of warning escaped from Rodriguez.

"She sounds lovely," Jackson commented and kicked again, but this time his ankles were caught in a steely grip.

"I wouldn't worry about her," Rodriguez chuckled, pulling Jackson down the bed and off the tailgate. Jackson landed on the hard, cold ground with a thud that rattled his teeth. "I'd be more worried about where you're going."

"Where am I going?" Jackson wheezed when Rodriguez's boot landed square in his stomach.

"I've got some old acquaintances who are eager to see you," came Rodriguez's cryptic reply. "Get up and walk. Don't make me carry your ass."

Rodriguez's rough hands hauled Jackson to his feet and a hand shoved him forward hard, knocking him to the ground again.

"Well, genius, this would be a lot easier if my feet weren't tied together," Jackson snarked from his new position in the snow.

"The only reason I'm not going to kill you right now is because I got a better offer to let someone else do it, Doc," Rodriguez hissed in his ear while he gripped Jackson's hair and wrenched his head back.

This is interesting. Jackson had no idea who would make a deal with the devil just so they could mete out the final blow themselves.

"I hope they make you suffer, you traitor. I hope it won't be an easy death like we gave your girlfriend," Rodriguez taunted.

Alicia. What happened to Alicia?

Jackson twisted in Rodriguez's grip, but only succeeded in ripping his own hair out. She couldn't be dead, she couldn't. The last time he'd seen her was with a look of terror on her face when the perimeter alarm went off.

"I guess you didn't know, huh? You were passed out the whole time when you got jumped like a little pussy in the hallway. You missed the whole fucking thing. She's still laying on the floor in your precious lab, her blood coating the tiles. What a waste, though … all that blood." Rodriguez's warm breath washed over the side of Jackson's face where the blindfold didn't cover.

A wave of relief rushed over Jackson when he remembered she had his blood in her system. It had only been a few days since he'd fed her his blood. If she died, she would just return as a Vampire. He didn't want that for her, but he would take what he could get … especially if she could use the serum she'd concocted to cure herself. Rodriguez was trying to rattle his chains, so to speak, goad him into a fight.

"Get on with it!" the woman screamed from the truck.

"She gets hangry," Rodriguez explained with a chuckle. An unladylike snarl came from the truck and Rodriguez let out a laugh. "Better do what the boss says."

Rodriguez pulled Jackson to his feet, but made no move to unbind them.

"She's not coming back," he laughed at Jackson's stunned silence. "Your girlfriend. Bullet to the heart. She's been lying on that floor for twelve hours," Rodriguez cackled as he dragged Jackson across the ground by the back of his shirt.

CHAPTER ELEVEN

Twelve hours.

Jackson hadn't seen the transition but a handful of times, but from what he *had* seen, the transition usually happened within an hour or two of the death of the victim. Twelve hours was much too long. A bullet to the heart would have stopped the transition. His relief had been premature. He played right into Rodriguez's hands … he got his hopes up Alicia had survived, just so Rodriguez could dash them into a million little pieces.

They may not have known each other long, but Jackson had a connection with Alicia he'd never felt with anyone before, not as a Hunter nor as a Vampire. When she was near, it was like gravity drew them together, telling them they belonged to one another. Jackson was never one to fall in love, quickly or otherwise, but this was a viable instance of 'when you know, you know.' And he had known. Alicia was his and he was hers. They belonged to one another, and now she was gone.

The pain of being dragged across asphalt barely covered in snow didn't register until Rodriguez stopped suddenly and dropped the collar of Jackson's shirt.

Jackson's head did a little bounce as it hit the pavement, giving him an instantaneous headache. The headache only got worse when Rodriguez pounded on a metal door and ripped the blindfold from Jackson's head with a dramatic flourish. The sudden onslaught of light—even just the moonlight reflecting off the snow—was excruciating paired with the pain in Jackson's head.

A little door inset in the main barricade slid open and Jackson could see a pair of eyes shift between where Rodriguez stood and Jackson lay on the ground. It was like something out of a mobster movie.

"Just open the fucking door," Rodriguez sighed impatiently. "You knew I was coming with him."

"You told me he'd be out when you brought him in," shifty-eyes challenged from behind the door.

"I can fucking break his neck again. I wouldn't mind one bit," Rodriguez offered, looking down at Jackson with a grin.

Scowling back in return, Jackson focused his attention on the surrounding building. It was a compilation of dull beige-toned brick. The metal door was rusted near to disintegrating along the edges. A lone yellowed security light shone above the entrance, highlighting stains that created the kind of artwork one might expect to find on a Rorschach test. This place was a shithole and Jackson had no idea what awaited him through the door. He could bet it wouldn't be anything good.

The door opened on creaky hinges, revealing a solidly muscled man Jackson had never seen before. Giving a thorough appraisal, Jackson tried to find a familiar trait to place a memory with the face, but came up empty. The man before him was built like a linebacker and looked like he might be able to give Jackson a run for his money if they were thrown in the ring in hand-to-hand combat. The guy was nothing but pure muscle with a scowl daring anyone to glance at him sideways. He narrowed his eyes at Jackson's obvious assessment and crossed his arms over his broad chest … no doubt emphasizing the pain they could bestow. If Jackson had still been human, he might have worried, but he wasn't and would always come out on top in a fight with a mere man.

"Bring him in," the gladiator growled, his eyes never leaving Jackson's.

"I said delivery to your door. Don't think for one second I'm stupid enough to step foot over that threshold into your domain," Rodriguez said with a little chuckle. "Bring him in yourself. Enjoy. I'll expect my payment to arrive tomorrow."

Nodding, the gladiator dropped his arms to his sides. His fists clenched and unclenched as if he was itching to pummel something with them. Jackson was pretty damned sure he knew what the guy's next target would be: him.

"Give him what a traitor deserves," Rodriguez sneered, then to Jackson, "Good luck, Doc."

Rodriguez turned on his heel and moved back to the truck. *My truck.* Jackson watched him round the front of the vehicle and wondered what new nightmare he'd been dumped in. Testing the chains binding him, he found they had no give. Not that he'd expected they would.

"Come on, turncoat, there are a whole lot of people waiting to see you."

The ominous words paired with the absolute disdain in his voice brought Jackson's attention back to the man at the door. Who would have such a dire need to see him that they'd make a deal with a demon like Rodriguez? A breeze blew across the parking lot, ruffling Jackson's hair and wafting the gladiator's scent to him. *A Hunter.* Now it was all starting to make sense. There were a whole bunch of *Hunters* waiting inside for him.

Fuck.

CHAPTER TWELVE

"Hey!" Jody yelled to accompany her pounding fist on the door. "We have to pee!"

The statement wasn't entirely untrue. She *did* have to pee, but she'd been deprived of hydration for the majority of her stay at Casa Vampire so it wasn't an emergency ... yet.

Footsteps approached and Jody took a step back right before the door violently swung inward, barely missing knocking her over. She was pretty sure knocking her out was the guard's intention.

The Vampire blocking the doorway scowled at her.

"We've been in here for, like, twelve hours and unless you want me peeing in a corner, I need to go to the bathroom," Jody demanded.

"I don't give a shit where you take a piss," the guard said, pulling at the door handle in an attempt to close it.

"Wait, please," Jody softened her tone. "Please?"

Jody tried to give him her best puppy dog eyes—widening them to project a sense of innocence or helplessness, whichever he chose to see. A chuckle escaped from the Vampire. He leaned forward so he was mere inches from her face, but Jody refused to back down and instead peered up at him coyly from beneath her lashes. Moving closer, he angled his face and brought his nose near to touching her neck. Jody closed her eyes and held her breath, waiting for him to strike with his fangs. He breathed in noisily, inhaling her scent through his nose, and let out the warm breath through his mouth, dampening the skin below her ear.

"You seem to be under the misunderstanding I have a death wish," he breathed out, each word a puff of warmth against her skin. Another deep inhale. "Those blue eyes tempt me, as does the thrum of the blood beating beneath your skin. Such a sweet scent." A soft groan escaped and echoed in her ear. He made a slight movement closer to where his lips barely caressed her neck, sending a sickened shudder through her. "Rodriguez has claimed you for his own," the Vampire whispered to her. "If I touch what is his, he will undoubtedly kill me. No woman is worth my life."

A surprised gasp escaped Jody when he planted his palm on her chest and shoved her backward into the room. Tripping over her own feet, Jody landed on her butt, clutching at her chest where he'd applied force. Giving her a smirk, he moved to pull the door shut, but Nora blocked the way. Jody was taken aback for a moment, as was the Vampire. Neither of them had seen or heard Nora move from the bed while the Vampire was enraptured with Jody's scent. Before the smirk could even slip from his face, Nora jammed something sharp up under his chin with a grunt.

Blood poured from the wound and the Vampire fell to the ground, his mouth agape and his eyes frozen wide. Jody slapped a hand over her mouth to quell the scream threatening to escape, along with the nausea rolling through her. Nora collapsed to the floor beside the body, her head making a dull thud against the linoleum tiles. Jody could guess she'd used the last of her strength to impale the Vampire. All so Jody would have a chance to escape.

"Nora!" Jody cried out, scrambling toward the fallen woman and avoiding looking at the corpse occupying the room with them.

Nora's eyes remained closed, but Jody could see the subtle rise and fall of her chest indicating she still breathed. Jody let out a small sigh of relief. They had a long way to go to get out of this, but at least Nora hadn't gone out with the Vampire. Jody needed all the allies she could get.

"Go find Endre," Nora whispered weakly.

"Let's get you on the bed first," Jody insisted, trying to pull Nora up over her shoulder and into a fireman's carry to get her to the bed.

Nora made an attempt at shoving her away, but it was feeble at best. "There's no time, just go find him," she asserted, pushing at Jody again.

Jody didn't really like the idea of leaving Nora on the floor, but she was right. There wouldn't be much time before the second guard came running or the rest of the Vampires returned. Scrambling to her feet, she glanced back at where Nora lay on the floor.

"Go!" Nora yelled hoarsely.

With one last look back, Jody sprinted through the doorway. She had no idea where to even begin to search for Endre, but her feet took her on the only path she knew—back toward the lab. She slammed into the wall as she turned a corner in the hallway, but the impact did little to stop her trajectory. When she made the second turn, she was careful to slow just enough so she didn't go careening into the plaster again. With the lab doors in view, she skidded to a halt before she reached them. Endre hadn't been in there when Rodriguez had her there the last time, so unless they moved him, he wasn't through those doors. Jody already knew what was there, and as much as she tried to convince herself to turn around and find another path to take, she took a step forward. It was like a car wreck; she knew it was gruesome, and yet she needed another peek. She told herself it was just to make sure Alicia was still there. Make sure her sister hadn't transitioned into a Vampire. A large part of Jody hoped she wouldn't find her body still lying on the floor.

She placed one hand on the doors, ready to push them open, but then paused. With eyes closed, Jody took in a deep breath to steel herself for the gore and the disappointment. One more breath. She nodded to herself and shoved the door open.

The sight before her was just as devastating as when Jody left it last. One headless Vampire corpse, another splayed across the floor, and Alicia. A wracking sob worked its way through her.

Alicia was still dead. She was really gone.

Jody would never see her get married or have kids. She'd never get to spoil her nieces or nephews with noisy toys Alicia would hate. If she made it out of this ordeal alive, she'd do so with a hole in her heart. The definitive loss of her sister brought Jody to her knees. She'd seen it many times at the hospital, families and loved ones crumpling under the weight of their grief. She'd never truly understood the sentiment until now. It was as if her body recognized the piece of her heart lying on the floor and lacked the will to carry on without it.

This was what Jody had needed, to see this and accept the finality of it in order to grieve. A cry from down the hallway brought her back to her senses. Nora needed her help. They needed to get out of here before Rodriguez and Jaqueline came back. Jody knew she shouldn't linger here any longer—she needed to find Endre—but still she couldn't turn away. She couldn't *walk* away. Her knees remained cemented in place and her eyes riveted on her sister's lifeless body, willing her to move.

It's easy, Al. Open your eyes and sit up. Open your eyes.

"If she hasn't transitioned by now, she ain't coming back," a deep voice said from behind her.

Every single muscle in Jody's body stiffened and her tears stilled. She was so stupid. She should have listened to Nora and found Endre. Instead, she had to come back here to stare at the shell that used to be her sister. Instead, she was right back in Rodriguez's clutches.

The heat of Rodriguez's body burned against her back where he stood only inches away. Jody waited for the violence, the rage at her attempted escape, failure though it was. His arm snaked around her waist and pulled her body up and back into his, slamming them together. His other hand wrapped up around her throat and gave a little squeeze. Jody drew in as much air as she could before it was cut off forever. But then his hand loosened, only to travel up to grip her jaw. He wrenched her head to the side so she could see him out of her periphery.

"It doesn't matter how long you stare at her, she won't wake up. You can't smell it, but I can ... the stench of death and decay," he whispered into her ear. He suddenly twisted her neck so she faced the body of her dead sister again. "She's decomposing right before your very eyes. Dead long enough for rigor mortis to set in. I bet she's already started to bloat."

"Stop. Please," Jody choked out between sobs. Visions of Alicia's body succumbing to the stages of decomposition were more than she could take right now. She wanted to remember Alicia whole, not as a puddle of flesh and organs.

"I want you to take a good look, sweetheart," Rodriguez told her through gritted teeth. "I want you to see what will happen to you if you even *think* about trying to escape again. Instead of your sister lying there, rotting away, it will be your worthless corpse. You're only worth leaving alive as long as keeping you around is less effort than killing you. You are mine to do with as I please. Do you understand?"

A broken cry accompanied Jody's nod of understanding.

"Do. You. Understand? I need to hear the word, sweetheart." Rodriguez's fingers dug into the flesh of her jaw.

"Yes!" Jody wailed.

"Good."

CHAPTER THIRTEEN

"Let's go, fucker," the gladiator grunted when he grabbed hold of the chains binding Jackson's hands.

"I think there's been some misunderstanding," Jackson protested as he was dragged through the doorway.

The metal door clanged shut behind him, ringing out an ominous note of finality.

"No one's asked my side of the story," Jackson continued, hoping to stay his execution.

"Shut up," the gladiator ordered, exertion evident in his strained voice.

The gladiator was a big dude, but so was Jackson; he could see how dragging him across a warehouse might wind the guy ... even with him being a Hunter.

"If you take these chains off my feet, I can walk myself, no need to throw out your back."

"I. Said. Shut. Up," the gladiator ground out, his fist cracking against Jackson's jaw.

"Fuck!" Jackson licked the blood from where his fang split his lip.

"Drop him here," another voice said.

Jackson turned his head to see if he recognized its owner. His stomach dropped at the sight that met him. There weren't just a few Hunters here. There was a large contingent—all with murderous glares meant just for him. A cursory glance counted twenty-one. He was going to get beaten down by twenty-one very angry Hunters.

The gladiator dropped him with a thud against the grimy concrete floor. Jackson had no idea what had been stored here previously, but it was evident it hadn't been fully cleaned up when the past owners vacated.

"I think there's been a misunderstanding," Jackson pleaded his case again.

"He just doesn't fucking shut up," the gladiator muttered with exasperation.

"You're not here to give an explanation, you're just here to bleed. Good Hunters died in those mountains because of you," another Hunter with a scar cutting clear across his face spat.

"Have at him, boys. Our very own breathing punching bag," the one Jackson pegged as the leader offered. He took a step back and watched with crossed arms as the mob of Hunters closed in on Jackson.

"Wait—" Jackson groaned when the first kick caught him in the ribs.

He took a right hook from another Hunter, breaking the bone around his eye socket. Another well-placed kick broke ribs on his left side, puncturing his lung. Jackson drew in a wheezing breath. Broken fingers. Busted jaw. Snapped ulna. Jackson cataloged each hit and each subsequent break. At this rate, they'd break every bone in his body at least once before they were through.

"This is for my brother, asshole," a Hunter Jackson couldn't see through his swollen eyes snarled.

The impact to his temple sent him reeling into darkness.

Pain radiated from every square inch of Jackson's body. He emerged from unconsciousness to find himself still lying on the warehouse floor, a pile of his own broken limbs. At least it seemed as though the Hunters had taken a breather when the last one knocked his lights out. Jackson could hear them a little ways off and it sounded like they were giving each other a play by play of his beat-down. As if they hadn't all been crowded around him either participating or watching. Well, at least his hearing was still intact. It was time to take stock of the rest of his body. He opened one eye, and then the other. They were both a little bit swollen, and the movement sent a sickening pain radiating from around his eye. Most of his bones had mended to the point where they remained fractures, but it would take a lot of blood to get him back into proper working order. He didn't see that happening any time soon.

"He's awake," a voice announced from across the room.

Jackson braced himself for his next ass-whooping, and was not disappointed. Everything which had mended during his little respite into the realm of unconsciousness was re-broken, plus the addition of a few more things. His throat was raw from the screams of agony he wasn't the least bit ashamed to admit ripped from him with every new break. He was also pretty fucking sure he had some fairly extensive organ damage.

One final hit—he couldn't even tell where anymore—overloaded his pain sensors and sent him tumbling back toward the abyss. He wondered how long they planned on doing this to him before they killed him. He was fairly certain he would be begging for death soon enough if the constant state of agony didn't subside.

"Take five, everyone," the leader called out just as Jackson sank into the depths.

Cold water splashed over Jackson's face, making him sputter and gasp for air. The sharp pain where a broken rib still punctured his lung threatened to take him back under. He'd lost track of the number of times they'd beaten him into unconsciousness, only to continue when he awoke. He stopped counting at six. Each session was more brutal than the last, the pain a constant hum throughout his body. He was beginning to wonder when his pain receptors would give up, and if it would be before the Hunters did. He *hoped* it was before, but he didn't figure luck or karma or any other mysterious forces would be on his side.

"Who's up?" the leader asked, addressing the group of Hunters now numbering closer to a dozen. Each of them sported split and bruised knuckles from their attentions.

"We made a cure," Jackson croaked out, coughing with the effort of both drawing in air and lending strength to his voice.

It was his last ditch effort to get them to stop. Maybe if he could give them something valuable, they might not kill him. The pressure his mind was under from their torturous beatings had led him down the road to desperation. His will was already as broken as his body, it was only a matter of time before his mind followed suit. He might as well throw out his ace in the hole and see if it caught someone's attention. If it didn't, he wasn't going to be any worse off. He didn't know if there *was* a worse off in this scenario. Jackson now knew how Prometheus felt—having an eagle swoop down and eat out his liver each day, only to have it grow back and the act be repeated day in and day out—however, he was hoping the Hunters weren't going to start cutting him open. He wouldn't put it past them. Though none of these guys seemed to fall into the same category of sick fuck as Rodriguez, from what he could tell, some of them weren't too far off.

"What'd he say?" one of the Hunters asked. Jackson didn't even bother opening his eyes to identify them. As far as he was concerned, they were all just an amalgamation of bringers of pain, their faces no longer mattered.

"I think he said something about a cure?"

"A cure for what?" they asked each other.

"A cure for what?" Now the question was directed to him.

"Vampirism," Jackson managed to get out before a coughing fit sending pain radiating through his entire chest took him over.

"Bullshit."

"He's delirious, throw more water on him."

"Yeah, then how come you're still a Vamp?"

"Mi—" Jackson started, then coughed. "Micelli killed her."

The thought of Alicia lying dead in the lab hurt more than all the physical pain these Hunters had inflicted upon him. He'd pinned hopes and a future on her. Not just her ability to bring him out of the darkness where being a Vampire slowly led him, but a future *with* her. He'd fallen for her, hard and fast. It was unlike anything he'd ever experienced before. Better than the high he got after a particularly satisfying kill. Sweeter than even the feeling of sinking into the warmth between her thighs. But where thoughts of a future with her filled him with warmth and happiness, the absence of that future filled him with pain and rage.

"Her?"

"Alicia," Jackson nearly sobbed. Even saying her name was agony knowing she'd never whisper his again.

"Who the fuck is this bitch Alicia?" one of the Hunters laughed, and Jackson wanted to tear his skull from his body.

"She," Jackson swallowed hard to stifle the emotion ringing clear in his words, "made the cure."

"There any truth to that?" the leader asked one of the others Hunters.

"Don't know," whoever he addressed responded.

"Find out what the hell Micelli was up to," the leader ordered.

"Why would you make a cure?" the leader addressed Jackson.

"Don't want to be monsters," Jackson croaked out.

"Bullshit!"

"Shut him the fuck up!"

A chorus of profanity and jeers sounded from the gathered Hunters.

"Shut up, all of you!" the leader roared, silencing the cacophony. "Until Sampson gets back with to me with some evidence of this cure one way or another, we're giving the doc here a breather."

Protests rang out from the group.

"Consider this your call from the governor," the leader informed Jackson. "We'll check into your story, and if what you say is true, you're going to help us inject every Vamp out there until we're out of a job."

CHAPTER FOURTEEN

The sound of broken sobbing roused Zeke from the darkness. The cries were far off, but the voice was unmistakable. *Jody*. The realization snapped him from the lingering haze he floated in. Opening his eyes, he took in his surroundings, gauging his chance of escaping. He appeared to be in a mechanical room of some kind. There were several boilers and some ancient-looking equipment he was unable to identify. Chains jingled in the dark expanse above him when he moved. A glance upward told him he was attached to a steel girder high in the ceiling.

Zeke pulled down on the chains, his muscles straining with the effort to break them, and only succeeded in pulling his body upward instead of the chains downward. He'd hoped the rusted appearance of his bindings denoted a weakness in the metal, but that didn't seem to be the case.

"I think your boyfriend is awake," a muffled voice chuckled from somewhere in the building above Zeke.

He cocked his head, trying to determine the direction of the voice and Jody's cries. It did him no good knowing where they were if he couldn't get to them.

"I've been waiting for him to wake up. I owe him some pain after our little scuffle at your house," the man said, presumably to Jody.

Zeke pulled harder on the chains. He knew now the voice belonged to the sadistic Vampire who'd tormented Jody when she'd been a captive in her own home. Zeke didn't want to think about the things he no doubt intended to do to her.

"Jody!" Zeke bellowed, hoping they were close enough and he was loud enough she could hear him. He needed her to know he was coming for her. He needed her to know he was still the knight to her damsel in distress until his last breath.

"He's calling for you, he can hear us up here," Rodriguez taunted. "Should we give him something to listen to, I wonder? Some entertainment while he hangs helpless, unable to save you? You made me look like a fool when your white knight butchered Kowalski and stole you away. This way I can torture you both at the same time."

A small whimper escaped Jody. The sound gutted Zeke. He needed to get to her.

"Do you know how acute our senses are, sweetheart?" Rodriguez continued, his voice further muffled by the clanking of chains while Zeke tugged feverishly at them. "Our hearing is so good, he'll hear the tearing of fabric when I rip your shirt open. He'll hear every suck when I bite into your tits. Oh, this is getting him worked up … me describing what I'm going to do to you. You want to hear more?"

"No," Jody sobbed.

"I wasn't asking you, sweetheart. You'll learn very quickly I don't care what you want. You live only for me now. Your life, your blood, your *body* belongs to me. You hear that, Zeke, was it? Your pretty little human whore is mine now." Rodriguez laughed.

Zeke growled in both anger and frustration. Sweat dripped down his face and soaked through his shirt with the exertion of tugging at the chains.

"He doesn't like when I call you a whore," Rodriguez chuckled. "But that's what you are now. *My* whore. Aren't you, sweetheart?"

The slide of skin across skin sounded, and Jody let out another wordless noise of pain.

"I expect an answer when I ask a question, *whore*. You're going to take everything I give to you, because you promised me *anything* to spare your life, and I intend to collect. Do you hear that, Zeke? You might want to rethink this one's loyalty. She jumped at the first chance to get my cock in her as soon as you were out of sight."

"Zeke!" Jody screamed, and the sound of the slap of flesh was unmistakable. A muffled cry followed the sound.

"He can't save you now," Rodriguez warned.

Frantic muffled screaming came from Jody, and red filled Zeke's vision as he imagined Rodriguez's hands covering her mouth.

"I usually reserve those screams for me," Rodriguez told her, "but we'll make an exception for your boyfriend. Maybe we'll even invite him up to watch one of these times."

Jody's cries became more insistent at the sound of tearing fabric and the familiar metallic clinking of a belt buckle. Zeke's struggle with his chains followed suit, the noise drowning out the sound of Jody's tussle with Rodriguez. As soon as Zeke got his hands on Rodriguez, he was going to rip that fucker's arms off for touching her.

Jody screamed into Rodriguez's hand covering her mouth, the connection slick with her tears. When his hand moved away, she screeched like a banshee, hoping to rupture his eardrum … but more than likely only succeeding in hurting her own. He mercilessly ripped through the knot she'd made at her waist with her borrowed scrubs, taking away the only layer of protection she had against his assault. The fabric whispered across her thighs and pooled around her ankles, further binding her for Rodriguez's sinister plans.

The clink of his belt unbuckling undid her. Her breaths came in hyperventilating gasps, quieting her cries while she struggled for air. Even without oxygen flowing freely to her lungs, she refused to quit fighting. She threw elbows and kicked her legs as best as she could with her traitorous clothing trapping her. Rodriguez's grip tightened around her waist and his now free hand clutched at her throat.

"Take it like a good little whore," he whispered, thrusting his hips forward.

Bile rose up from her empty stomach when she felt his erect cock slide along the inside of her thigh.

"Minion!" Jaqueline's voice snapped behind them, and Jody had never been more glad to hear that horrible woman speak.

A low growl emanated from Rodriguez, sending vibrations through Jody. "Don't call me that."

A little smirk lifted the corner of Jaqueline's lips.

"Put your dick and your little slut away, for fuck's sake," Jaqueline admonished. "We have work to do, you can play with your toy later!"

Rodriguez took deep breaths, but his hold on Jody didn't ease. His body shook with barely concealed rage, sending answering tremors through her. He swung both of them around to face Jaqueline. Her eyes scanned up and down the length of their bodies, clearly unimpressed with the display before her.

"Be a good boy and put your toy away and meet me in Endre's room. I have someone else you can hurt for a while," she sighed, her voice bored. "Now."

Rodriguez flung Jody to the floor. She landed with a hard impact on her hip, the frigid linoleum on her bare ass and thighs sending shivers through her. Pulling up her scrubs, she scrambled backward a safe distance when he stalked menacingly toward Jaqueline. She folded her arms and looked down pointedly at his naked groin. He followed her gaze then gave Jaqueline a smirk.

"I think you're jealous because your pussy's the only one here I have no desire to fuck," he sneered.

"I'm not jealous. I'm just reminding you of your place." Leaning toward him, she narrowed her eyes.

Jody scooted farther back away from them. She wasn't too keen on the idea of getting between the two of them arguing. Rodriguez shot her a furious look that froze her in place.

"Don't go anywhere, sweetheart, you and I have unfinished business," he warned.

"You will put her back in her room and do as I command," Jaqueline demanded.

"I don't take orders from you anymore," Rodriguez sneered, turning from her to fully face Jody, his raging erection still on full display.

Jody's eyes grew wide with terror, and she scrambled backward on hands and knees until her back hit the wall. Rodriguez's hand shot out and grasped a fistful of hair. She cried out as strands pulled loose from her scalp. Yanking her to her feet, he slammed her back against the wall, pinning her there with his naked hips. She was grateful for the barrier the scrubs provided, thin as it was.

"You seem to forget you're only here because of me. You owe me your *life,*" Jacqueline shouted. "If it weren't for *me*, Micelli would have never even known where to look for you. If it weren't for *me*, you wouldn't get to have your revenge on Nora and the Hunters. Everyone. If it weren't for *me*, you'd be *dead*!"

"I've helped you get what you wanted, I don't owe you anything."

"Endre is still alive. You've done nothing to help me," Jaqueline hissed. "Nothing."

"Nothing?" Rodriguez asked doubtfully, holding Jody up between them.

"Except continually fuck your little playthings. You don't get to claim them all as your own. You aren't the only one who wants revenge," Jaqueline pointed out.

"This one is mine," he said, shaking Jody's head by her hair. She tried not to wince in pain, but it was impossible. "Nora is mine. You can have Endre. I don't give a shit about him."

"I want Nora. I want that little bitch to suffer for taking what was mine," Jaqueline countered.

Rodriguez laughed. "No. She's not up for negotiation. That little cunt killed me ... almost for good."

"Then I want her," Jaqueline said, her eyes turning to meet Jody's. A devious smile crept over her face, and Jody found it hard to believe she'd had drinks with her as friends before all this.

The argument was so surreal, it was hard for Jody to wrap her head around. They were fighting over which of their captives they felt they had a right to torture and kill. This nightmare just continued to get worse and worse.

"Mine," Rodriguez growled.

"Then put your toy away before I *take* it away," Jaqueline ground out through gritted teeth.

Jaqueline turned on her heel and stomped out of the room, leaving Jody alone with Rodriguez again. He wrenched her head back by her hair, straining her neck and making it hard to swallow down the tears welling up.

"Don't worry, I won't let her take you away. We're going to lock you up safe and sound, and when I've taken care of her, we can finish what we started," he whispered low in her ear.

Rodriguez made quick work of refastening his belt, and then with a violent yank, Jody was thrown over his shoulder. The impact of his shoulder into her midsection knocked the wind out of her. She spent the journey through the maze of hallways back to the room she shared with Nora just trying to pull in a breath. When they approached the door, he let out an irritated sigh before stepping over the body of the dead guard, no doubt cataloging another infraction Jody would be required to repent for.

"You just leave a mess wherever you go, don't you, sweetheart?" he said, tossing her onto the bed. "Stay."

Jody landed with a bounce, but thankfully it wasn't enough force to launch her from the bed. She watched as Rodriguez strode over to the guard and shook his head. He kicked the body into the room, out of the way of the swinging door—completely ignoring Nora where she still lay on the floor beside her victim. Jody scrambled from the bed toward Nora, the need to ensure she still breathed overriding the survival instinct to obey Rodriguez's order.

She'd almost reached Nora when Rodriguez stepped into her path. He shoved her with such force she stumbled backward, falling into the bed. Before she had time to react, Rodriguez had hold of her wrists and pinned them to the mattress on either side of her head. He pressed his body lewdly into hers, grinding his cock along her hip.

"I'm going to enjoy fucking the defiance out of you." He ran his fangs along her neck, leaving little cuts and trails of blood.

Rodriguez licked along the cuts, collecting the droplets with his tongue. Jody gagged on the vomit rising in her throat at the feel of his tongue on her. After a drawn out moan, he pushed himself away, leaving her to take in slow breaths to keep from throwing up. On his way out the door, he gave Nora a kick to the ribs.

"I'll be back soon, ladies. Maybe we can get a little two on one action going," he said with a wink before pulling the door closed behind him.

CHAPTER FIFTEEN

Endre stretched his jaw, moving it from side to side. It had taken much longer to heal without an infusion of blood, but at least he could open his mouth now.

"I wouldn't get too used to that feeling," Rodriguez warned as he strode into the room.

His visit was expected; Endre had heard the little spat between Rodriguez and Jaqueline in the lab. It seemed Rodriguez wasn't nearly quite as far under her thumb as she'd believed. Endre hoped to capitalize on their power struggle to get out of these bindings and get to Nora.

"How long are you going to let her talk to you like a misbehaving dog?" Endre jeered.

Rodriguez chuckled. "I may not look like the brightest crayon in the box, but I'm definitely smart enough to know your game. You won't manipulate me. We won't bond over a mutual hatred for the ice queen. So save your breath, it won't work."

"So, you're doing all this because she told you to?" Endre pushed, trying to jam his barb as far under Rodriguez's skin as possible.

"Nope. I'm doing this because I love doling out pain. I'd prefer to save it for your woman, but I doubt she'd be as much fun now that she's a weak and pathetic mess on the floor." Planting his feet apart, Rodriguez shoved his hands in his pockets. "I take it by the expression on your face, you don't know just how bad off she is."

Endre tried to school his expression into an impassive one, but what use was it, really? They all knew Endre was hopelessly in love with Nora and would rain down fiery retribution on anyone who laid a finger on her. Starting with this asshole.

"I struck a chord there, didn't I? See, I know all about manipulation," Rodriguez proclaimed with a sick grin. "But the time for talk is done, I'm ready to shed some blood," he chuckled, then shoved a piece of cloth in Endre's mouth to quiet him.

"Always so much talking. Never enough action," Jaqueline's exasperated voice filled the room.

The metallic click of the safety being flicked off a gun sounded in the room as she strode up behind Rodriguez. Endre watched on with a grim sense of satisfaction while she pressed the barrel of her pistol into the back of Rodriguez's head.

"I'm sorry, Rod, you're just too much of a liability," she sighed with mock sadness.

He looked up thoughtfully at Endre. "I wondered where the ice queen had run off to."

"Do you really think it's a good idea to insult me when I've got a gun pressed to your skull?" Jaqueline hissed at him.

"Do you really think it's a good idea to bring a gun to a knife fight?" Rodriguez questioned, winking up at Endre, his hand flexing in his pocket.

Jaqueline furrowed her brow in confusion. "That's not how it goes."

"It does now," Rodriguez announced as he spun, knife in hand.

Rodriguez left no room for hesitation. His blade sliced through Jaqueline's throat with no preamble. The sickening sounds of tearing flesh filled the room as he made quick work of separating head from body. The scent of blood filled the air and Endre fought back his demon. Rodriguez had no such qualms.

"Fucking bitch," he spat, as her body crumpled to the linoleum.

He tossed her head where it landed with a squelching smack next to the still body. Rodriguez ran his tongue across the bloody blade, his eyes fluttering closed when he swallowed. A loud crashing noise sounded from somewhere below, interrupting the expression of serenity masking the creature he usually wore. A snarl ripped through him, and he aimed his glare at Endre, then his blade.

"Your bitch is next," he proclaimed. "I'm going to let you listen to her scream. Then I'm going to finish you off and get out of this hellhole."

Endre struggled against the straps holding him to the table, but just like the other thousand attempts he'd made, they didn't loosen one iota. That's why they were here … because they were Vampire proof.

Rodriguez stalked from the room, blade at the ready, toward Nora.

Zeke gave himself only a fraction of a second to celebrate finally working the chains loose from the ceiling and free from his arms. He'd endured enough of listening to Rodriguez threaten Jody, his fury fueling his determination to get free and kill that fucker.

Launching up the stairs three at a time, he raced through the hallways toward where he'd last heard Jody's voice. He was surprised to find the corridors empty. It wasn't until he turned the corner when he finally ran into a guard. The fight was anticlimactic, taking Zeke only ten seconds to disarm the Vampire and shoot him in the heart with his own gun. He counted. When the guard's body fell to the floor, Zeke was already at Jody's door.

With a deft twist of his wrist and a shove with his shoulder, Zeke burst into the room. Jody screamed when the doorjamb splintered, sending debris flying across the room toward where her and Nora perched on the bed. Zeke stood in the doorway, panting heavily, his gaze sweeping the room for any lingering threats. When his eyes landed on Jody again, he felt all the tension melt from his body.

"Zeke," she whispered in relief.

Crossing the room in two strides, he scooped her off the bed and enveloped her in his arms. She buried her face in his chest and her body shook with wracking sobs that splintered his heart.

"You're safe now, princess. I've got you, you're safe," he whispered into her hair, stroking it gently. "Come on, let's get you both out of here."

Reluctantly he pulled away from Jody, but he couldn't stop touching her, reassuring himself she was alive and unharmed. Cupping her face with both his hands, Zeke lost himself for a moment in the watery depths of her blue eyes. Warmth filled him when the corners of her mouth turned up into a small smile.

"My knight in shining armor," Jody sighed.

Unable to hold back any longer, he pressed his lips to hers in a chaste kiss. "I'm never letting you out of my sight again," he proclaimed against her lips before taking her mouth in a feverish kiss.

He'd almost lost her and he never wanted to feel that devastation again. Absorbed in the moment, he swiped his tongue across her bottom lip, demanding entry. Jody didn't disappoint. Their tongues tangled together, tasting one another. A throat cleared from behind Zeke and he reluctantly broke away. A glance over his shoulder revealed Nora feebly trying to sit up on the bed.

"We have to go," Jody declared, rushing from his arms over to Nora.

Nodding his agreement, Zeke tamped down the lust burning through him after getting a taste of Jody. Taking one look at Nora, he blew out a breath. If this was what the cure did to them, he couldn't say he was eager to take it. He'd find a way to deal with the thirst rather than be reduced to the weak and broken state Nora was in.

"Can you walk?" he asked her.

"She can barely talk," Jody whispered from beside him. She looked down at Nora, sympathy in her eyes.

Scooping Nora into his arms, Zeke headed for the door. The longer they lingered, the less their chances were of getting out of there alive.

"Endre," Nora croaked out, barely above a whisper.

"Let's get you safe first. I'll come back for him," Zeke promised, hoping he could keep his word.

Zeke stepped into the hallway carrying Nora, Jody at his back. Their escape was immediately hampered by Rodriguez's form guarding the corridor. He leaned casually against the wall with his arms crossed, a bloody knife gripped in one hand.

"Going somewhere?" he asked, raising his eyebrows. "You wouldn't happen to be trying to take my girls with you, would you?"

CHAPTER SIXTEEN

"Sir," *a* *loud* voice jarred Jackson from his fitful slumber on the concrete.

"What did you find?" the leader asked.

The warehouse had been quiet for the last few hours; just the occasional shuffling of feet and conversations in low tones while the Hunters gathered information. The sudden enthusiasm in the Hunter's voice drew everyone's attention, including Jackson's.

"I was able to pull up the surveillance video from the tail we put on Micelli."

"And?"

"And it looks like Doc is telling the truth. The woman he referred to, Alicia, is one Alicia Matthews, Biomedical Engineer. Micelli met with her a few weeks ago and offered her a job. The video doesn't indicate what exactly the job was, but she rejected the offer. Turns out, Micelli doesn't like to hear no for an answer. A few days later, one of our guys caught wind of a Vamp prowling around outside her office. Something scared the Vamp away, but a few nights later, the girl goes missing. Georgio checked out her apartment, the place has been torn apart. Blood on the floor, evidence of a struggle."

Jackson couldn't help the little laugh bubbling up from him, thinking about how irritated Alicia would be to hear them refer to her precious condo as an apartment. The surprising sting of tears pricked behind his eyes and he swallowed hard to tamp them down.

"Bring Doc in here," the leader ordered.

The clomping of boots drew near to where Jackson lay.

"Boss wants to see you," the gladiator said, gripping the chain around Jackson's wrists.

Even the small movement of his arms sent pain racing along his nerve endings. He couldn't hold back the bellow of pain that burst from him. At this rate, he would pass out again before they got him over to the built-in office area.

"Sir?" the gladiator called out to the leader.

"What is it?" the leader demanded, exasperation clear in his tone.

"He isn't healing, sir. Everything's still busted up."

The leader swore a blue streak then yelled out, "Grab a blood bag from the back."

They had Jackson's attention now. They were going to give him blood, and from the sounds of it, there was a whole store of bags somewhere in 'the back.' The Vampire in him automatically worked on devising a scheme to get at the blood, but he forced it down. There was no way he was going to be able to trick his way out of this. These guys were Hunters, and he knew how Hunters were trained. They would see right through him if he tried to pull one over on them.

"We're going to give you a little blood. Only a little, just to heal the breaks," the leader advised, crouching down above him. His head blocked the light of one of the industrial fixtures in the ceiling and Jackson could barely see his face in shadow. "But," he continued, "you have to answer a few questions first."

Jackson should have known it wouldn't be that easy. He should have known he wouldn't get something for nothing from them. They held all the cards here, he just needed to tell them what to lay down to win.

"Sounds like a fair deal," Jackson wheezed through his punctured lung. He couldn't wait to get that thing healed up—along with whatever other organ was currently spilling out fluids inside of him. He was pretty sure there was some damage to his spleen.

Another Hunter tossed a bag over to the leader, and he caught it right in front of Jackson's face.

"That girl, Alicia, her apartment was trashed," the leader started.

"Condo," Jackson corrected. He couldn't help himself.

"What?"

"She hates … hated when people called it an apartment," he explained with a dry laugh, which sent him into a coughing fit.

"Did you trash her *condo*? Take her prisoner to help with this cure scheme?"

"Rodriguez," Jackson rasped, "he was trying to drive her to run to the lab."

"I don't get it," one of the other Hunters mused. "I thought Micelli wanted her to help him? Why would he scare her to you?"

Jackson gestured with his chin to the bag in the leader's grip and let out an exaggerated cough ending in a painful wheeze to illustrate his need for that blood. The leader pulled a knife from his pocket and cut a slit in the top of the bag.

"Open up," he ordered.

Mouth open, Jackson closed his eyes and waited. He didn't care how much they gave him; even a few drops would help ease the pain and quench some of the thirst that had been slowly gnawing at him. A stream of the cool liquid hit his tongue and he relished every drop. He wasn't used to taking his blood cold—it changed the taste a little—but he wasn't about to complain to a pack of Hunters about the delicate bouquet this particular vintage was missing because it had been refrigerated.

Swallowing down the small mouthful he was allowed, Jackson savored the replenishing feeling coursing through his veins. He tried to concentrate to direct the blood to his ribs first, to mend them and get them the hell out of his lung, but he didn't know if that was even a thing. It seemed it didn't need to be a thing, because his body already knew where the direst injuries were and directed the blood's healing energies to his broken ribs. He grunted as his ribs set themselves and the long, arduous process of mending bone began.

"You have to admit, that's fucking incredible," one of the Hunters breathed, clearly in awe as they watched Jackson's body put itself back together.

"Vampire blood administered to a human heals just as fast," Jackson commented. His voice was stronger than it was before and lacked the whistle at the end of each breath. "There are some pretty fucked up side effects if the subject dies when the blood is in their system, though."

"So that's how it happened," the leader muttered, scratching at the stubble on his chin. "To you and Rodriguez. All we got was his side of the story, but it seems to me there's more here than what he led us to believe."

"Sounds like a story for another time," Jackson acknowledged, hoping he'd have the opportunity to set the record straight-er.

It wasn't as though he could ever deny he'd helped a Vampire, their sworn enemy, of his own volition and ended up essentially being an accomplice to the destruction of a whole facility with more than a few Hunters still inside. Jackson hoped to get back on track with the story about Micelli; he needed to convey to them the urgency of distrusting Micelli and Rodriguez and changing the direction of their operation. He finished giving the parts of the story he knew, right up until the invasion in the lab and having his neck broken.

"That's quite a tale there, Doc," the leader commented uneasily after Jackson had finished recounting the events of the last several weeks. Then he turned to the gladiator. "Check out the details and tell me where our tail is on Micelli. I want to know what that two-faced son of a bitch is up to."

Crossing his arms, the leader scowled down at Jackson. Jackson tried not to scowl back.

"Fuck, I don't know what to do with you." The leader sighed, running his hands through his hair and tilting his head up to the ceiling, as if looking to the heavens for the answer.

"You could loosen these chains, for starters," Jackson suggested, gesturing down to the chains still binding his wrists.

"Fat chance of that happening, Doc. I don't know what to make of you." When Jackson responded with a look of confusion, he continued, "You were a Hunter, but you helped a Vampire escape from a secure facility, leaving a few dozen men dead in your wake. Then, you transition into a Vamp yourself and help the other Vamps come up with a cure. Why?"

"It all kind of just happened," Jackson replied with a shrug, thinking back to his first encounter with Nora in the bunker.

"That's bullshit and you know it," the leader countered, his arms crossed over his chest again.

"Have you ever just stopped to think that what Hunters do might be wrong?" Jackson questioned, hoping to appeal to this guy's sense of curiosity.

Instead the Hunter narrowed his eyes dangerously at Jackson. "I didn't either," Jackson continued, shaking his head, "until I met her."

"The engineer? Alicia?"

"No, the Vampire. Nora," Jackson clarified.

"We saw the footage of that Vamp. One of the finest women I have ever seen. Most of us here figured it all started with thinking with your dick and forgetting she'd bite the thing off."

Jackson couldn't help the chuckle that escaped. He remembered the effect Nora had on his libido the first time he set eyes on her. It all disappeared for him when he saw the way she gazed upon Endre and how he shared that look of love absolute.

"She was quite something to look at. But her womanly assets weren't *really* what I was interested in. It was her blood. I watched her heal from a wound like it was nothing. I was fascinated by the way the Vampire body worked … especially the blood. I figured for an enemy we've fought for centuries, we sure don't know a whole hell of a lot about them," Jackson admitted.

"Didn't need to. All we needed to know was where to aim to take one out," the leader stated, shrugging his shoulders.

"I started to experiment with her blood, to see if I could get it to regenerate cells in a human—or Hunter—as quickly as it did for a Vampire. I used it to heal Rodriguez."

"You fucking *experimented* on Rodriguez?" the leader spat.

"I saved his life," Jackson protested. "He would have died if he hadn't gotten the Vampire blood."

"But now he's a Vamp."

"And so am I."

"You experimented on yourself?" he asked in disbelief.

"Did you know the blood holds memories?" Jackson offered, steering the conversation in a different direction.

"Say what now?"

"When Vampires drink blood, they can see memories from when the donor's blood was spilled, or when they spilled the blood of someone else," Jackson recounted.

"Don't try to class it up, Doc, by calling your victims 'donors'."

Jackson continued as if he hadn't been interrupted, "The same goes for when a human, or Hunter, drinks the blood of a Vampire. Not only does it heal the body, but you can also see the memories in *their* blood."

"Why are you telling me this, Doc?"

"Because, I ingested Nora's blood and I saw her memories. In those memories I learned that just like humans, just like *Hunters*, there are the good and the bad. We hunted Vampires and exterminated them indiscriminately. We never bothered to learn who they were," Jackson said.

"They're *Vampires,* they kill people. *You* kill people."

"But what kind of people?"

"You're not doing a great job pleading your case here, Doc," the leader warned, shaking his head and taking in a deep breath. "And I'm losing my patience with this conversation."

"Nora was hunting violent criminals. Murderers. Rapists. Child Abusers. *She* didn't kill humans indiscriminately. She chose to hunt along the bottom rung of society. And she was working with Endre on a *cure*," Jackson argued emphatically. "Does that really scream 'monster' to you?"

The Hunter took a step back and shook his head.

"Don't you see? They were trying to come up with a cure because we, Vampires, know the demons within we fight against each day and we know what happens when we let them win. We came up with a cure because we don't *want* the demon to win."

"Fuck," he answered, scrubbing his hands down his face.

"By aligning yourself with the likes of Rodriguez and Micelli, you're enabling the ones who want the demon to win," Jackson pointed out.

"Rodriguez used to be one of us. Micelli *is* one of us."

"Micelli's a Hunter?" Jackson couldn't help the question from bursting forth. It was news to him.

"Yeah, he came to us. Told us if we helped him find you and your lab, we could have you. He seemed a little sketchy, so we kept our eyes on him while we looked out for your lab. We weren't going to pass up the opportunity to get our hands on you," the leader told him.

"So what's it going to be?" Jackson questioned.

"What the fuck do you mean what's it going to be?"

"Are you going to unchain me and help reclaim the lab so we can make more of the cure, or are you going to kill me?" Jackson asked, partially because he wanted to get the idea out there and partially because he needed to know if he was going to be walking out of this warehouse alive.

"Sir?" another Hunter interrupted before Jackson could get his answer.

"What?" the leader barked, clearly annoyed with the interruption.

"We have no eyes on Micelli, he's no longer at the lab. But there's something going down there. There've been gunshots reported," the Hunter detailed.

Jackson closed his eyes and a sick feeling rolled through him. He already knew Alicia was one of Micelli's victims, he didn't want to think of who else had died on his orders.

"All right, let's get a team over there."

"Yes, sir."

"You," the leader barked, looking down at Jackson, "are coming with. For whatever goddamned reason, I believe your cockamamie story. If I discover one lie in all this, I'll dispatch your manipulative ass myself. Understand?"

"Are you going to unchain me?" Jackson questioned, proffering his bound hands.

"Your feet, yes. I'm not carrying your ass anywhere. You'll have to earn the hands."

"Fair enough," Jackson agreed, just glad to be able to feel his feet again.

The clinking of the chain links hitting the floor once his ankles were released was music to Jackson's ears.

CHAPTER SEVENTEEN

Nora clutched onto Zeke's shirt, trying desperately to get him to put her down. She always thought of herself as a strong woman, even after the demon in front of them tortured her. She had survived all he'd done to her and was able to move on with her life. But seeing him alive after she had reveled in his death at *her* hands broke something loose inside of her. Her body trembled with fear at just the sight of him. Never mind as soon as he opened his mouth, his voice sent her into full on tremors. Nora most definitely didn't feel strong anymore, not in body and certainly not in spirit. All her instincts told her to flee, they told her to get as far away from Rodriguez as fast as she possibly could. Those instincts even overrode her desire to ensure those around her remained safe.

Zeke's grip on her tightened, but he didn't move any closer to Rodriguez. He may not know the hell the sadistic Vampire put her through, but he sure tuned into her trepidation. Which meant Rodriguez had, too. Now he knew she was absolutely petrified of him. She was exactly where he wanted, a quivering mess of unstable emotions.

"Sweetheart, what did I tell you would happen to you if you tried to escape again?" Rodriguez scolded, picking at his nails with the tip of his knife.

When no one answered, his piercing gaze flicked up and bored into a spot somewhere behind Zeke—on Jody. Nora heard Jody's breath hitch and her heart race. At least she knew she wasn't the only one who lost her shit as soon as Rodriguez showed his face. Not that that was a particularly wonderful bonding experience with someone.

Pushing Jody behind him, Zeke slid Nora down to the ground at his feet. Nora breathed a sigh of relief at moving out of Rodriguez's direct line of sight. All it would have taken was one well-aimed throw of that horrible knife to end her. Or Jody. Or Zeke. *What is he waiting for, which game is he playing now?* If she'd learned anything in her short stint in his company, it was that he didn't do anything without a purpose. He was methodical, devoid of emotion when he carried out his favorite violent pastimes. There was an eerie calm he adopted even when performing gruesome tasks like flaying the skin from her back. But he was deadliest when his emotions got the better of him, breaking through that controlled veneer. Right now, he donned the impassive mask which hid the brutal calculation happening beneath. If something didn't happen soon, it was only a matter of time before the calm and control slipped and the vicious animal locked away broke free.

Rodriguez tilted his head to the side and made a sweeping assessment of Zeke, who stood with muscles taut, anticipating a strike.

"You're outmatched here, you know that, right?" Rodriguez pointed out, turning his angry gaze to Zeke. "Physically, I've got you beat. And I can bet you haven't got the training I've got. You've also got two damsels to keep away from me. How're you going to protect both of them?"

He examined the blade of his knife with a practiced nonchalance, but Nora knew better. She just hoped Zeke did, too. Rodriguez was waiting to make his move, ready to pounce at the first sign of hesitation or weakness.

"I'm still deciding which of you to kill first."

Nora could see the wheels turning in Zeke's head, trying to find a way out of this that didn't result in her or Jody getting hurt—or killed—and Rodriguez on the floor in pieces. It was an impossible scenario, as far as Nora could see. Her pessimism bloomed fierce as she evaluated the scene. She could foresee no instance where they all walked away alive and Rodriguez lay dead … at least not with Zeke being the only one defending them. From what she knew of Jody, it wasn't in the woman's nature to give up, but she was simply no match for the likes of a Vampire. And neither was Nora. Not anymore. If she had still had her strength, she would have stood beside Zeke, ready to take down the bastard who continued to cause her trauma. But the simple fact was she wasn't strong enough anymore.

Taking a step over Nora, Zeke fully blocked her from Rodriguez's wrath. She was grateful for the barrier and the protection, especially from someone who didn't know her at all. He held all the markings of a good man, and a good Vampire. She really hoped he came out of all of this alive.

"Volunteering as tribute, eh? Isn't that how you all say it up here, sweetheart? Eh?" Rodriguez chuckled, tilting his head to get a better view of Jody behind Zeke.

"Nah, that's a few more hours north," Zeke answered in an attempt to draw Rodriguez's attention from Jody.

Rodriguez held his hands out to his sides and pinned Zeke with a glare. "What are you waiting for, huh? Trust me, you don't want me to make the first move. I'll let you in on a little secret, I play dirty. *Real* dirty. Just ask Nora, or your girlfriend back there," he said with a wink, his tone brimming with innuendo.

He was trying to bait Zeke, get him to strike in anger, but luckily Zeke was smart enough to see right through it. Zeke's level head gave Nora a sense of hope. If he could get Rodriguez to lose his temper, there was a greater chance Rodriguez would get sloppy and give Zeke an opening.

"All right," Rodriguez relented, shaking his head.

In one swift movement, Rodriguez sent his blade sailing end over end through the air ... aimed exactly where Jody's face peeked out from behind

Zeke's broad back. The knife seemed to move in slow motion and Nora's reaction time was even slower. By the time she opened her mouth to warn Jody to move, the blade sunk inches into muscled flesh.

Jody screamed when her body collided with the floor as Zeke shoved her, and Zeke let out a grunt when the metal dug into his shoulder when he stepped into the knife's path. Rodriguez didn't waste any time to allow for recovery from either shock or injury, and charged the distance of the corridor toward Zeke with a roar.

Blade still protruding from his shoulder, Zeke barreled toward Rodriguez, putting a few feet between where the two Vampires clashed and where Nora and now Jody sprawled on the linoleum. The hallway filled with sounds of fists on flesh and animalistic growling. The two big men traded blows, trying to get the upper hand, and it was a horrific sight to behold. The force of the blows broke bones and skin alike, sending shouts to echo through the hallway and blood to spatter the walls.

Wounds healed quickly, but were almost immediately replaced by new ones. The blurring movement was dizzying, sending a wave of nausea through Nora. She wanted to avert her gaze, but the brutal display was mesmerizing. Rodriguez was larger than Zeke by a degree, but somehow Zeke held his own with sheer ferocity. Nora attributed his fierceness to fighting for his life and the life of two others he'd taken upon himself to protect.

Zeke let out an agonizing, guttural growl as Rodriguez grabbed hold of the handle of his blade and twisted. With a well-aimed hook, Zeke dislodged the larger Vampire and pulled the blade from his shoulder, tossing it behind him into the hallway. The blade skittered across the linoleum tiles, sliding to a stop just inches from where Nora lay paralyzed, a spectator for the most gruesome brawl she'd ever witnessed. Rodriguez and Zeke continued to pummel each other, but Nora's attention was now focused on the blade, as was Jody's.

Jody crawled across the floor toward Nora and the knife. She glanced up at Nora before snatching it up off the floor, but before she could pull away with it and do something stupid, Nora grasped her wrist to keep her still. Jody looked down in surprise, but didn't try to pull away. It was brave that Jody wanted to help, but it was also stupid.

"Run. Now. While they're occupied," Nora ordered.

"I can't just leave him," Jody said, her eyes shining with unshed tears. "He saved my life. And I can't leave you."

Nora shook her head. "Now's your chance … your only one. If Zeke dies, we all die. Go!"

Jody still made no move to go. Nora wasn't going to let her waste her life by jumping into the fray.

"Zeke would want you to run," Nora implored in low tones. She knew it was true. The expression on Jody's face said she knew it also. "He jumped in there so you could get away," Nora speculated, stating it as fact.

Jody shook her head, tears escaping the corners of her eyes. "I'm not a coward."

"You're not stupid either. Go," Nora pressed.

"I can't leave you here, he'll kill you, Nora," Jody protested.

Nora squeezed Jody's wrist with her remaining strength. A gasp escaped Jody and she looked down where they touched. Nora may be weak, but she was weak for a *Vampire*, not a human. She was still stronger than Jody by a small degree, so there was little hope of Jody breaking her hold. Jody released the blade and Nora dropped her wrist in relief; there were already enough broken bones in this hallway. Snatching up the blade, she stared Jody down with as threatening an expression as she could manage. She may not really be a Vampire anymore, but she could still exude menace with merely a look.

Jody scrambled to her feet and ran toward the end of the hallway. When she disappeared around a corner, Nora brought her attention to the grappling Vampires. Rodriguez's attention was focused on where Jody made her hasty escape. He shoved Zeke backward, the glint in his eye murderous as he watched his prey make her getaway. Zeke stumbled back a few feet, nearly tripping over where Nora lay. She did her best to scramble out of the way but wasn't fast enough.

Zeke toppled to the floor beside Nora, and Rodriguez followed, landing atop him. The hits to Zeke were swift and merciless. Rodriguez pummeled Zeke relentlessly, delivering hits to his major organs, eliciting grunts of pain.

When Nora regained her wits, she did her best to lunge at Rodriguez's back, blade in hand. It wouldn't take much force to drive the blade into the soft parts of him. Throwing all her weight and strength behind the movement, she plunged the knife into his left kidney. It wouldn't kill him, but she didn't need to deliver the killing blow to divert his attention from Zeke for long enough for Zeke to get into a more advantageous position.

Rodriguez let out a roar and the back of his hand struck Nora across the cheek, the force of the blow enough to knock her backward. She fell to her back, taking the blade with her, as well as Rodriguez's attention.

"Fucking bitch, wait your turn," he growled. His eyes burned with rage and hatred concentrated solely on her for a moment before turning back to Zeke.

The moment Rodriguez turned back to face Zeke, his fist connected with Rodriguez's jaw. Nora heard the revealing snap of bone breaking. The blow, however, didn't deter Rodriguez's assault. A new sound rang out in the hallway when, with a quick jerk of his hands, Rodriguez snapped Zeke's neck. Zeke's limbs fell limp to the floor with a dull thud.

Nora's eyes widened with terror. With slow, deliberate movements, Rodriguez climbed to his feet. He towered over Nora and a devilish smile curled the corners of his lips. He re-situated his broken jaw with one hand and held out the other toward Nora.

"Well," he announced with a smirk, "looks like it's just you and me now." His gaze flicked down to the blade still clutched in Nora's hand. "I'm going to need that to finish the job." He curled his fingers in a beckoning motion, impatience coloring his features as he waited for her to hand him her murder weapon.

CHAPTER EIGHTEEN

Jody panted with exertion as she tore through the halls. She hadn't been too keen on the idea of leaving Zeke and Nora to fend off Rodriguez, but she knew Nora was right—sending her away was the smartest course of action. However, where Nora had most likely intended for Jody to flee the building and begin life anew outside it, Jody had other plans.

Her feet skidded to a halt down a corridor she hadn't had the opportunity to explore in her limited time in the lab. The hallway was lit with a single florescent bulb at the other end, the remaining lights either burned out or merely turned off. She had no idea if there were more Vampires lurking in the shadows. There was only one Vampire Jody needed to find, she just had to pick the right door.

Steeling herself with a deep breath, Jody continued on; there wasn't time to waste with thoughts of what the shadows concealed. She needed to find the one person left who could take on Rodriguez. It wasn't that she didn't think Zeke could hold his own, but two against one were always better odds, and if going down this unnerving hallway meant the difference between

Zeke's survival and death, she was damned well going to do it.

The first door creaked on the hinges as she flung it open. An empty room. The next one was some kind of closet. Despair started to fill her as each subsequent room did not hold what she searched for.

"Endre, if you can hear me, make some noise," Jody breathed out. Not sure why if she wanted someone to hear her, she was whispering.

A loud clattering came from the room at the very end of the hall and she rushed toward it, hoping it was Endre through the door and *not* another Vampire leading her to her doom. Jody flung open the door, trying to grasp what the dim light revealed. Jaqueline lay in two parts on the floor painted with blood. Her body lay with limbs sprawled in awkward positions, but her head lay a few feet away, an unrecognizable mask of gore.

Cold sweat broke out over Jody's body and her stomach lurched. She clutched at her shirt to keep the vomit from rising in her throat. It didn't do any good. Dropping to her knees, she retched on the floor, heaving up only bile from her empty stomach. She wiped the back of her shaking hand across her mouth, wishing for some water to wash away the acrid taste.

Her eyes once again lit upon Jaqueline's body and she turned away quickly before she made a repeat performance. Movement to her right caught her eyes and she saw her salvation. Or what she hoped would be her salvation.

A man was strapped upright to a table, struggling against the bonds. He furrowed his brows at her and mumbled incoherently around something shoved in his mouth. Jody struggled to stand on trembling legs and moved in for a closer look. Upon closer inspection, she stared into the face of a fucking Viking. She didn't recognize him, but she'd bet everything she owned this was Endre. The realization spurred her into action.

Jody first pulled the gag from his mouth, then immediately started searching for the clasps for the straps.

"Zeke and Rodriguez are out there beating the shit out of each other," she told Endre while she undid the first clasp.

"Where is Nora?" Endre demanded, his tone rough but lined with concern.

"She's still out there," Jody lamented, shaking her head. Three straps down, two to go.

A growl erupted from Endre, and Jody wasn't sure if it was directed at her or the situation. She hoped it was the situation. She didn't want to think she'd come this far and survived so much violence only to be devoured by the Vampire she was trying to set loose.

The strap holding down Endre's arms came free, and he shoved her out of the way while he unclasped the remaining restraints.

"Get out of here," Endre ordered Jody as he launched himself from the table and out the door.

A part of her wanted to listen and just get the hell out of dodge, but the larger part of her rebelled against the idea and followed after Endre. He was fast, so there was no way she could hope to keep up with him, but she knew where he was going. She just hoped they wouldn't arrive too late.

Nora tried to hold back her terror at being alone with her tormentor again. He stood before her, hand still outstretched with the expectation she was going to give up her weapon and the slim possibility of getting out of this alive. Not a chance.

"Ever the fighter, hmm?" Rodriguez taunted, breaking into a broad grin. "That's all right, you know I like it when you fight me. I've got to get a few screams out of you anyway, so I can keep my word to your lover."

Rodriguez lunged toward her, his hand swiping at hers to grab the knife, but she moved it quicker than he'd expected and caught him between the ribs. He glanced down at his new wound in surprise, before looking back to her face. His expression of astonishment dropped and was replaced with a terrifying smile. He leaned in toward Nora's face, his hand now at her throat, pushing the metal farther into his side. His heavy body pressed her into the floor, leaving no option of escape, her hand pinned between them still grasping the knife handle.

"I never did get to fuck you," Rodriguez whispered in her ear, his grip constricting her throat. "I want him to hear you scream when I tear into your pussy. Then I'm going to cut your throat open wide and watch your blood paint the floor. When I'm done with you, I'm going to tear Endre's head off with my bare hands. I've always wanted to try that."

A low growl built in her chest and Nora tried in vain to twist the blade. She wanted to give him a little additional pain before he inflicted more on her. He ground his hardness against her hip and Nora held back tears of rage. There was nothing worse than feeling helpless, and that's exactly what she was pinned beneath Rodriguez, not even able to move the hand between them.

A loud roar sounded from down the next hallway and thundering steps that shook the floor drew near. Rodriguez looked up, a deep scowl written on his face. A familiar scent assaulted her nostrils and she nearly broke down into tears with relief. *Endre.*

"I didn't realize you wanted to watch," Rodriguez quipped to the incoming Endre.

Rodriguez rose to his feet, taking Nora with him, the knife still planted between his ribs momentarily forgotten. He slammed Nora against the wall by her throat, her head hitting with enough force to see stars.

"I've been waiting to do this," he chuckled, then plunged his fangs viciously into her neck.

It wasn't gentle in the least; the pain was excruciating. Nora let out a deafening scream, but was silenced when the grip on her throat tightened. She already felt weak before Rodriguez started feeding from her, now dark spots started to creep their way into the edge of her vision, taking dizzy to a whole new level. He hummed with pleasure while he continued to pull mouthful after mouthful of her blood.

Nora started to lose focus and her sense of time. *What was taking Endre so long?* She wondered if she'd hallucinated his scent. She'd been so relieved thinking he was coming for her, and now she realized he wasn't.

Sharp fangs ripped through her flesh in one instant, and then the weight of Rodriguez was gone the next. Without him holding her standing, she slid down the wall to the floor, amazed by the sight before her. Feral snarling brought her eyes open, and for the second time that day, she witnessed a brawl in the hallway. It was almost like an instant replay of the one between Rodriguez and Zeke earlier, but this time Endre was in Zeke's place. At least she hadn't been hallucinating.

"Zeke! Oh my God, Zeke!" Jody shouted when she turned the corner.

Jody sprinted down the hall and her gaze made contact with Nora's. Nora should have known the woman was too damned stubborn to save her own skin.

She was glad she'd freed Endre, but now she'd put herself in danger … again. Jody didn't break pace, but dropped violently to her knees when she came to where Zeke lay on the ground. Tears swam in her eyes while she looked down at him helplessly. The unbridled emotion on her face nearly got Nora's tears flowing.

"His neck is broken, he'll recover," Nora croaked out; the bite in her neck was painful and made speaking difficult.

Nora almost forgot she wasn't a Vampire anymore and her wounds wouldn't heal nearly instantaneously. She put a hand up to the wound, to stem the flow of blood, surprised to see she still gripped Rodriguez's knife. She transferred the blade to her other hand and pressed against the torn flesh.

"Fuck that hurts," she groaned.

"Nora, you're bleeding," Jody exclaimed, her expression dumbfounded. She scrambled over Zeke to where Nora sat. "Let me see it," she ordered, attempting to pull Nora's hand away.

"I told you to get out of here," Nora whispered painfully. *Stubborn woman.*

"Don't try to talk," Jody commanded, glancing over at where Endre and Rodriguez still battled.

Nora's gaze followed, her brows pinched with concern. Couldn't Rodriguez fucking die already? She already thought she'd killed him once, only to have him reappear and threaten the lives of her and everyone she cared about. The evil son of a bitch just needed to *die.*

"Here." Holding out her hand, Jody looked down at the blade.

"No," Nora croaked, shaking her head. The movement increased her vertigo which only increased the nausea.

"I have an idea." Jody gestured wildly for the blade. Nora laid the blade in her hand, eying her warily. "Do you think he'll mind if we borrow some of his blood?" she asked, biting her lip and glancing down at Zeke's prone form.

The idea started to take shape in Nora's head. It was worth a shot. She didn't think Zeke would mind, as long as it meant he got to wake up. The blade hovered hesitantly over Zeke in Jody's hand. Then with a sigh, she drew it across his forearm. Nora braced herself for the familiar bloodlust that had been her constant companion for months now, but was please to find it absent. It seemed there was hope for this cure yet. Maybe a little bit of tweaking, but it at least abated her hunger.

Without a moment's hesitation, Nora leaned down and licked the droplets of blood from Zeke's arm. She might not be a Vampire anymore, but he was, and his blood would heal her and hopefully give her back some of her strength. Nora swallowed down the blood, finding the taste not nearly as pleasant as she once had. The coppery tang caught her at the back of her throat, nearly causing her to gag. The sudden sensation of her fangs elongating was alarming. She'd assumed with the administration of the cure, they'd remain dormant or something.

Jody gasped from beside her when her fangs made their appearance. It would certainly make drinking from Zeke a little easier. Nora latched onto his arm and drew in several mouthfuls, comforted with the familiar feeling of new blood mingling with her own. By the time she pulled away and wiped the blood from her lips, she felt like a new woman. The wound at her neck was closing up, and her strength was coming back.

"Stay with Zeke," Nora ordered, climbing to her feet. It was her turn to hold her hand out for the blade.

Jody gave it up readily, her gaze turned up to where Nora stood. Her brows furrowed with concern, but she didn't protest.

"Kill that fucker," Jody whispered, pulling Zeke's head to rest in her lap.

With a nod, Nora turned to where Endre and Rodriguez had crashed through the drywall into one of the adjoining rooms. She peeked into the hole they made and staggered backward when a body came hurtling toward her. Letting out a surprised shriek, she barely managed to avoid the impact. The flurry of movement made it difficult to tell where one Vampire ended and the other began. Nora watched carefully, waiting for an opening where she could take down Rodriguez with his own blade. Her eyes were still sharp and followed their movements, but each move was unpredictable, so she couldn't begin to estimate where the next strike would land and where she should be to ensure Rodriguez took the brunt of it.

It felt like hours, but was likely only a few minutes, before an opportunity presented itself. She finally caught Endre's eye and he once again drove Rodriguez toward the opening in the wall where she stood. The other Vampire seemed unaware of the trap waiting for him.

When he was within arm's reach, Nora thrust the blade into Rodriguez's back, aiming for his heart. She had no qualms about stabbing him in the back if it meant he would never haunt her again. Rodriguez bellowed and reached an arm behind him in search of the weapon. Nora took that to mean she'd missed his heart, just like she had the first time she thought she killed him. She'd hoped she wouldn't make the same mistake twice, but seeing as she had, perhaps the third time would be the charm. Nora pulled the blade from his back and Endre treated him to a right hook, preventing him from turning around to take his rage out on Nora. Taking aim, she stabbed the knife into Rodriguez's back again, fairly certain this time it would hit its mark.

Another bellow sounded from her enemy and he dropped to his knees. She'd wanted to see the expression on his face when she killed him .... again. But sometimes in life, you didn't get everything you wanted. Nora pulled the blade from his back with a brutal yank, and his body slumped forward, head hung but breaths still pulled into his lungs.

"Love," Endre warned, but she wouldn't be placated.

Nora once thought she'd put the nightmare that was Rodriguez behind her and had been mistaken. This time, she wasn't taking any chances. Gripping his hair as tightly as she could, just as he'd done to her countless times, she yanked his head back. When she jerked on his hair, she had hoped to hear the snap of some bones—she'd even settle for cartilage or connective tissue—but it seemed Nora still wasn't up to full strength and may never be. His breath came out in a wheezing gasps and his eyelids drooped heavily. She imagined a lifetime of evil deeds could exhaust a person.

"Burn in hell," she spat at him, looking into those dark, soulless eyes for the last time.

Dragging the razor sharp blade across his neck, she was glad to be standing behind him and out of the spray. It was liberating to see his blood gush from the wound, like a flowing crimson symbol of her freedom. She would make sure there was no coming back this time. The blood flow began to wane, and she cut across the wound again and again, mesmerized by the sight of it. It was like déjà vu, killing him again—wanting desperately to see the light leave him just so she knew she'd be safe from his torment.

Strong hands grasped Nora's shoulders, stilling her movement to make yet another cut in the mangled flesh. The hands traveled down to hers and took the blade from her shaking grip.

"Take his head off, make sure he can never come back," she choked out.

With the efficient movements of a warrior from centuries past, Endre sliced through the remaining flesh on Rodriguez's neck. Nora still held onto his hair, the head now weighing heavily in her grip without a neck to support it. The body slumped to the side. It took all her willpower not to hurl her enemy's head across the room. Instead, she unclasped her fingers from the short dark strands and let it fall to land on his unmoving chest. It was done. Rodriguez was gone. For good.

Revenge had sapped all the strength from Nora and she collapsed back into the strong figure holding her upright.

"I've got you," Endre reassured, wrapping his arms around her and leading her from the carnage. "He can never harm you again."

CHAPTER NINETEEN

Jackson walked up to the building that had served as his home for the last few months, sandwiched between two Hunters who were in charge of keeping tabs on him. The chains clinked every time he moved his arms, but it seemed he was the only one they were bothering.

"The door is all clear," a Hunter announced into the headset. Jackson wasn't wearing one, but he could damn well hear it in stereo from the guys flanking him. Which meant anyone inside could hear it, too.

"Hold up," the leader ordered.

Jackson made a mental note to get the guy's name once this was all said and done—without him, Jackson would still be lying in a puddle of his own fluids and broken bones on the floor of that warehouse. Granted, he wouldn't have been there are all if it weren't for the Hunter, but he wasn't about to point that out.

The leader turned to Jackson. "How many are in there?" he demanded, though no one seemed to know who he was asking.

"We don't have a clear visual," one of the Hunters announced. The leader just raised his eyebrows and waited for Jackson's input.

"I've got four heartbeats," he remarked after listening for a moment. Dark dread twisted in the pit of his stomach. Only four. Who did they belong to? Which of his friends had he lost?

The leader looked at him doubtfully.

"I swear there are only four. I get what happens to me if you find out otherwise, but I'm telling the truth," Jackson swore.

"Human or Vampire?"

"I can't tell who they belong to, only that they're there," Jackson confessed with a shrug.

There were almost two dozen Hunters stationed in various strategic locations around the building. He didn't think they were worried about being outmanned or outgunned.

"All right, go," the leader commanded the group.

The back door of the building opened on silent hinges, the alarm long since disabled from Micelli's initial invasion. It was likely Rodriguez was too stupid or too arrogant to set up a new one. A small contingent of Hunters moved through the main hallway, swarming and clearing each room. When the entire hallway cleared, Jackson was moved inside with the rest of the crew.

The team moved around the corner and shouting erupted.

"Drop your weapon! Get down on the ground!"

Jackson tore off down the hallway, despite the protests of his guards and the warnings that he would get shot if he didn't play by their rules. The faint scent of Alicia wafted through the air and Jackson hoped beyond hope Rodriguez had been lying when he said she was dead.

When Jackson turned the corner, he stopped short. The corridor was destroyed beyond recognition. Plaster was strewn about the floor and the walls had holes and dents in them the size of people. Blood spatter marred the otherwise pristine white of the paint, signaling the violence that had taken place here in his absence.

"Jesus," one of the Hunters next to him swore.

Jackson followed his gaze to the decapitated form of Rodriguez. He felt nothing but relief at the Vampire's death. His gaze swept over to the figures lying on the ground, complying with the Hunter's orders of submission. He could hardly believe his eyes. Nora, Endre, Zeke, and a blonde woman he assumed to be Jody lay sprawled on the floor, each of them with a heartbeat. Four. There was no Alicia. Jackson inhaled the air again, the scent of Alicia stronger where he stood. Then it hit him like a punch to the gut. It wasn't Alicia he smelled, it was Jody. It would make sense they would have a similar scent since they were sisters.

Despair settled over Jackson. Rodriguez had told the truth. Alicia was gone.

"What the fuck happened here?" the leader asked, gaping at the destruction around them. "Who are they?" He gestured to the figures lying on the floor.

"Nora, Endre, Zeke and Jody," Jackson recited, nodding to each one of them in turn.

"Where's Rodriguez?"

"Right here, sir," one of the Hunters offered, pointing with his outstretched gun toward Rodriguez's body.

"Fuck. Where's everyone else?" the leader asked.

"A sweep of the building is complete," the gladiator announced.

"And?"

"We found several more bodies," the gladiator reported.

"Any of them Micelli?"

"No, sir."

"Where's Micelli?" the leader asked, directing his question to their new captives.

It was Alicia's sister, Jody, who spoke up. "He had some kind of seizure after he was injected with the serum. He was catatonic for so long, I thought he was dead. Then something happened, he had a violent episode, and fled," Jody's muffled voice reached Jackson from where her face was buried in her hands.

He was almost glad he couldn't see her face. Her hair was the same color as Alicia's, he could only imagine he'd see the family resemblance in her features when he finally looked upon her face.

"*Micelli* did that in the lab?" one of the Hunters asked, aghast.

Jody nodded in response.

"You know anything about this?" the leader questioned Jackson.

Jackson shook his head. "They had me unconscious for a while … knocked me back out every time I woke up."

The leader snorted, probably at the parallel to the situation the Hunters had him in for the last several hours.

"All right, what do we got here, folks?" the leader asked, directing his question to the group of Hunters surrounding them. "Good guys? Bad guys?"

"Nora and Endre worked with me in the lab," Jackson started before the leader pegged him with a hard look.

"No one asked you, Doc," he replied, a scowl forming between his brows. He turned his gaze to look expectantly at the gladiator.

"Sir, the dark-haired female matches the description of Nora Ellison, the college student who disappeared in Italy last summer."

Huh. Jackson had never known what Nora's last name was.

"That you?" the leader asked, nudging Nora with his toe.

Endre let out a low growl which could not be mistaken for anything other than hostile. The sound of several firearms being directed at Endre's back echoed throughout the corridor.

"Yes," Nora answered weakly. The lack of strength in her voice worried Jackson.

"She sick?" someone asked.

"She was injected with the serum, it doesn't seem to be functioning entirely as intended," Jody answered.

What? They hadn't gotten the chance to test it out. They weren't supposed to partake until it had been tested out on one of Micelli's goons they'd captured. Jackson supposed that changed rather quickly after Micelli stormed the gates, so to speak.

"You the spokesperson for the group?" the leader prompted, nudging Jody to roll over, earning a growl from Zeke.

Interesting.

Blonde hair and vivid blue eyes looking eerily similar to Alicia's assaulted Jackson's senses. He knew he'd break as soon as he saw her. His chest tightened painfully and he had to remind himself how to breathe. He forced himself to, taking in deep breaths to keep his heart rate steady. The Vampires in the hallway would hear the change, but it was unlikely the Hunters would detect it.

"I guess so," Jody said in a small voice.

Jody's gaze darted from Hunter to Hunter and the weapons they trained on her. As if she was a threat. She was the least threatening of the four of them, but Jackson knew they wouldn't care. As far as the Hunters were concerned, all Vampires and those associated with Vampires were dangerous.

"What's your name, sweetheart?" the leader asked, staring down at the woman.

Jody visibly flinched at the endearment. Jackson recalled it was a favorite of Rodriguez's and he was fairly certain she'd been called that by him on more than one occasion.

"Jody Matthews," she answered quickly.

"How do you fit into this puzzle, Jody?" the leader demanded, staring down at her where she lay on the floor, his stance intimidating.

"Um," Jody began, biting her lip and glancing around like she didn't know where to begin.

"She's Alicia's sister," Jackson spoke up, unable to endure the look of discomfort on her face. It was too similar to Alicia and he just wanted it to go away.

"Ah, the engineer who developed your serum," the leader acknowledged, pursing his lips and nodding knowingly.

"Micelli held her captive in her home as a bargaining chip with Alicia so she would infiltrate the lab and move the cure along," Jackson filled in when Jody seemed to be frozen with fear. The leader gave Jackson a raised eyebrow, so he continued, "I called Zeke to recover her and bring her back here."

"Zeke, huh?"

"Ezekiel Collingwood, pronounced deceased as a result of a vehicle wreck a few months ago," one of the Hunters recited.

"Vampire," the gladiator announced with venom lacing his tone.

"I'm sorry to interrupt, but are you going to kill us?" Nora croaked out, rolling to her back with a wheeze.

Endre was immediately at her side, hands touching her face, checking her pulse and generally fussing over her.

"No. Doc here told us about your cure, so we wanted to have a look for ourselves. See if we could administer it to the Vampire population in general, but it looks like maybe you've got a few kinks to work out." The leader nodded down to Nora's emaciated form.

"If you're not going to kill us, what are you going to do with us?" Jody questioned.

Jackson noticed the other Vampires had remained especially quiet, no doubt plotting an escape plan or mass murder ... maybe both.

"Depends on how well you cooperate with us and if your stories check out. From the intel we've gathered, I'd say we might be able to come to a pleasant working arrangement for everyone involved. You get to keep your lab, perfect your cure, and we'll distribute it. By force if necessary. We'll call it a truce. An alliance for a common cause," the leader proposed, giving a toothy smile.

"Who are you?" Jody inquired, looking between the leader and Jackson who still stood bound in chains.

"Hunters," the leader answered simply.

Jody's eyebrows furrowed in confusion. Jackson could bet she'd figure out what exactly they hunted, but he didn't want to leave anything open to interpretation.

"Vampire Hunters," Jackson clarified.

Jody's gaze swung over to him, and at first it was laced with pain and sadness, then flashed with anger. Jackson could see the blame burning in her eyes. He was supposed to keep Alicia safe. He was supposed to keep her *alive* and he'd failed.

CHAPTER TWENTY

"So, what do you say? Do we have a deal?" the lead Hunter petitioned.

All eyes turned to Endre and he let out a long sigh. He'd already let one Hunter-turned-Vampire and then a human invade his lab, what was an army of Hunters? He was naturally suspicious they would turn on him as soon as he finished figuring out what Alicia did to his formula and fucking redo the whole thing so no one else ended up wasting away like Nora. His choice was made for him. If he wanted to save Nora, he would have to ally himself with the Hunters.

Endre's gaze moved to Nora's profile. While he still lay face-down on the linoleum, she stared up at the ceiling. He listened to her heartbeats and grew more and more concerned with each passing moment. They were slowing, she was deteriorating at a highly accelerated rate, and unless he was given the chance to figure out how to help her, she was going to die. And if Nora died, every Hunter in this building would die a most painful death for keeping him from helping her.

"I will help with reformulation of the cure, but I have conditions," Endre demanded, rising to his feet.

He'd be damned if he would cower on his back like a dog submitting to these Hunters.

All weapons were immediately aimed at him, but he paid them no mind. His attention was focused on the mouthpiece for this gathering of Hunters.

"I don't think you're in much of a position to make demands," the mouthpiece tsked.

"If this is an alliance, and not an occupation, I demand equal freedom," Endre expressed, raising his eyebrows at the Hunter in challenge. He could not claim to have a mutually beneficial arrangement and hope to maintain complete control. That wasn't something Endre would stand for.

"Done," the Hunter acknowledged with a nod. "Lower your weapons," he ordered his soldiers.

The Hunters reluctantly lowered their firearms, more than one of them shooting nervous looks Endre's way.

"Also," Endre continued, reaching down to pull Nora into his arms from where she still lay on the floor, "Nora will require treatment and evaluation before I can continue. I will need to determine where the flaws were in the serum. This will take some time. The lab is in shambles and is in no condition to house work."

"Get your woman taken care of," the mouthpiece told him.

Endre couldn't help but chuckle at how Nora bristled at statement. He had a feeling this Hunter would learn in due time, as soon as he brought Nora back to proper health, 'his woman' was not to be trifled with.

"My men will provide cleanup. We will be staying on the premises as long as is required for the adjustments to the cure, so get used to our presence," the Hunter warned. "All right, men," he said, addressing the Hunters around them, "first order of business is to bring the bodies down to the incinerator."

A feeling of both gratitude and frustration filled Endre. The Hunters would be cleaning up the mess, but would also be invading his space indefinitely. The facility had once been a small hospital, so it had enough rooms to house them all, but Hunters and Vampires sharing the space was a recipe for disaster.

"We're going to need you two to remain here as well," the leader told Jody and nodded to Zeke. Endre was relieved Nora would still be able to remain close to her new friend. He didn't feel isolation would do her any good in her state right now.

The leader of the Hunters began walking away, barking orders at his men on the areas most needing cleanup and which men were to be stationed in which quadrants of the facility. Endre lost interest in their din and directed his attention to Nora. Her eyes had slipped closed in a deep sleep. Her breathing and heart rate were steady, but sluggish. He needed to move her to their room so he could examine her more closely in the privacy of their quarters.

"Wait!" Jody called out, scrambling to her feet after the big military looking dude started shouting at all the Hunters.

He stopped and turned to her, his brow marred by deep furrows. "What can I help you with, Miss Matthews?"

Zeke had migrated to her side and laid a possessive hand on her hip. Jody tried not to let butterflies go into a frenzy in her stomach, but it was hard not to when he was near. She needed to keep her mind on the task at hand. They were going to burn the bodies. *All* the bodies.

"Can I please just say one final good-bye to my sister?" Jody managed to choke out.

She'd already seen Alicia's body on several occasions now, but it was always in shock and with the hope she'd see her sister come back, even if it was as a Vampire. Now, she needed the finality of a good-bye so she could let the hope go and move on to mourning the loss of a beautiful woman's life cut tragically short.

"I'd also like to say good-bye," a voice said from beside her—opposite where Zeke stood.

Jody turned her head and took in the man she knew was Jackson, though the Hunters continued to call him Doc. They seemed to be familiar with him, but Jody didn't understand the connection. In truth, she didn't really care to know, she was already deeper into this dark otherworld of creatures than she had ever imagined, she didn't need to delve into their histories as well.

Taking in the dark hair and dark eyes, Jody wouldn't have cataloged him as striking, but she could see the allure and why her sister would have been smitten with him. Judging by the break in his voice, he had returned Alicia's affections. But still, where was he when she was shot? Why wasn't he there to protect her? It was his fault her sister was dead.

Jody gave herself a shake. No. She knew better than that. She'd seen the blame passed around from person to person in families sitting in waiting rooms to hear the news of their loved ones passing. These things happen sometimes. Sometimes people just meet a tragic end, their time come too soon. She'd offered such soothing placations to others in times of need, but somehow they didn't work the same on her. She would not be calmed, she would not send her grief to be absorbed into the atmosphere. She was angry. There was no reason for Alicia to die. Her mind tugged at her, whispering to her what she already knew … *Jackson isn't to blame.*

He would have saved her if he could have—the look in his eyes and the sound of pain in his voice told her that—but she still needed someone to blame, someone to rail at. Some tangible *thing* she could inflict the pain of the hollow ache in her chest upon. Though, none who surrounded her were the culprits that brought death so early to her sister's door. Alicia would not have even stepped foot in this lab had it not been for Micelli. *He* was the one to blame. He was the true monster in all this. And he was not here to receive her anger.

The leader of the Hunters nodded solemnly, understanding their need to say a final farewell. An incinerator is not how Jody would have chosen to honor her sister, but knowing Alicia, it would be exactly how she would have wanted to go. Even so, Jody couldn't stomach the thought of burning her with those who had taken her life. It seemed a great dishonor to treat her just as her murderers were being treated.

"Please don't burn her with them," Jody pleaded, hoping they understood the sentiment and didn't just see an emotional woman pleading for something trivial.

"Of course," the Hunter acquiesced, bowing his head.

"Thank you," Jody acknowledged. He understood. It was easy to read in his eyes. She would bet he'd buried or burned more than his fair share of bodies in his lifetime.

The Hunter moved so he no longer barred their way, and Jody and Zeke walked past him. Jackson followed behind, the quiet clink of chain links trailing him. That wasn't going to fly. Jackson had helped them all, it wasn't right he was still bound. She may not know much about the Vampire, but if he'd earned even a smidge of affection from Alicia, he had to be a good man. And right now, she needed him, just as sure he was going to need her when they said their final farewells.

Stopping abruptly, Jody turned to the Hunter who had been more accommodating than she could have ever hoped for. "Are those really necessary?" she asked, looking pointedly at Jackson's chains.

The Hunter seemed to mull over the idea of leaving Jackson clapped in irons, but with a deep, resigned exhale, he pulled out set of keys and removed the shackles.

"Thank you …" Jackson responded graciously, hesitating as though he was waiting for the Hunter to fill a void.

"Gustafson," the Hunter replied, his voice gruff.

"What about Micelli?" Jackson asked, stopping Gustafson when he turned to walk away.

Micelli. Jody longed to get her hands on the creature and strangle the life from him. It was more than he deserved—a death with more pain would be preferable. Though, the method wasn't really what was important, Jody just wanted to see his rotting corpse. She wouldn't be the one doling out his punishment; there were others more capable who would take the honor, she could be sure of that. Without a doubt, Jackson wanted to be first in line for the task. Jody had never pegged herself as a vengeful person—usually the calming voice of reason—but her grief was screaming for blood, Micelli's blood.

"I'll send a party out to exterminate him," Gustafson conceded.

"I want to pull the trigger," Jackson ground out, his voice thick with emotion.

Gustafson narrowed his eyes and assessed Jackson critically before blowing out another resigned sigh. "Fine, you will go as part of the extermination contingent," he allowed, his voice full of warning. "On one condition."

"Name it," Jackson approved without hesitation.

"You operate as part of the team and you follow *my* orders," Gustafson stipulated.

Jackson nodded. "Yes, sir."

"All right," Gustafson sighed, the tension in his shoulders relaxing. "Go say good-bye to your girl, then we move out."

CHAPTER TWENTY-ONE

It was difficult for Jackson to look at Alicia. From the description Jody gave, it sounded as though he was lucky he was seeing her laid out on an examination table instead of on the floor slowly decomposing in a pool of her own blood. He didn't want to remember her that way, the victim of a grisly murder. This way, seeing her arms folded over her stomach, he could almost imagine she was in a deep sleep.

"It's so strange," Jody commented, slipping her hand into Alicia's.

Jackson only wished he was brave enough to touch her. The moment he did, though, he would feel the cold of her skin and know the illusion was just that.

"What's that?" he murmured, placing a strand of hair so it lay perfectly across Alicia's forehead.

"There's no rigor mortis," Jody laughed nervously.

Jackson felt it, too—the need to expel the emotion in some way. If he didn't, it would continue to build inside of him until he exploded. But where Jody laughed and evaluated Alicia with the mind of one who frequently witnessed death and recognized its signs,

Jackson would save his grief and let it build until he was face-to-face with Micelli. Jackson had no intention of killing the beast Micelli had become with a bullet, that was too kind. No, he would render Micelli limb from limb and watch his blood soak the ground, not even worth enough for him to feed upon. Micelli had stolen his future, and that was unforgivable.

Jody murmured heartfelt good-byes to her sister and Jackson tried not to listen, but it was impossible. They were beautiful and only made him want to find new ways to torture Micelli. When it was his turn, Jackson told her corpse he would avenge her. He told her about the future he'd imagined they could have had, all the while, Jody watched him. Jackson didn't care if she saw him break. She needed to know Alicia had been loved. Even if it had been a short affair, it had been real.

"Time to go," Gustafson announced quietly from the doorway, regret both in his tone and on his face.

Jackson understood the need to move quickly, but it didn't make the pain of walking away from Alicia any less. They had yet to pinpoint Micelli's location, and once found, they had to find a way to either capture or kill him without drawing significant attention. He had a feeling Micelli wouldn't be too hard to find. Surely wherever he went, a trail of bodies followed.

IRREVERSIBLE

Squeezing her sister's cool fingers one last time, Jody pressed a kiss to her forehead before leaving the room, seeking Zeke's comforting arms to collapse into. Jackson walked past to follow Gustafson, a look of determination on his face. Jody put her faith in Jackson to carry out the revenge Alicia deserved. His words to her dead sister showed her just how much he'd come to care for her in their short time together, and Jody could relate. The situation was not so unlike her and Zeke.

Zeke held Jody while she cried into his shoulder, soaking his shirt with salty tears. He was a pillar of strength when she needed it and she was eternally grateful. Standing outside the lab, they waited for the Hunters to take Alicia to the incinerator in the basement. Jody needed to be there, she didn't want Alicia to be alone when it happened.

Great sobs shook Jody's shoulders, the noise carrying down the hallway. She didn't care who heard them. They were the sound of loss and heartbreak. Her sister had always been her best friend, a piece of her no one else could ever fill.

Trailing behind Gustafson, Jackson absently followed each turn down the hallway to the lab's newly acquired armory. His thoughts were admittedly elsewhere, the image of Alicia lying cold, waiting for cremation burned into his mind. He was certain it was that gruesome image, rather than any blood memory, which would haunt him for the rest of his days. He'd lost many people he cared about in his life—family and comrades alike—but none of those losses pained him as deeply as the loss of Alicia.

"Doc, if you want to go with the team, you need to get out of your head and into the game. From the video we pulled from your security system, it looks like Micelli is damned near rabid. You might have an advantage over him in several ways being a Vamp, but he's still deadly. Especially if you aren't focused," Gustafson cautioned, not unkindly, as he patted Jackson's shoulder with a heavy hand.

A nod was all Jackson could provide in response. He didn't think Micelli would have to worry about not having his undivided attention. As soon as he set eyes on the devil, Micelli would be the *only* thing Jackson would be able to think about.

"All right," Gustafson remarked to Jackson with a loud exhale, then turned to the group of gathered Hunters.

Taking in each face, Jackson gauged whether he would be shot dead by these Hunters as soon as he was off the premises. He hoped not, but didn't entirely brush aside the possibility. He was the very epitome of the things they hated—a Vampire and a Hunter seemingly without loyalty. In the end, it didn't really matter. As long as Micelli ended up in the ground, Jackson didn't care all that much if he walked away or not. Endre could get on with the lab and reformulating the serum without him. Jody hardly knew him, and Zeke he could see being a little bummed, but he was actually concerned with how Nora would take things if he wound up dead. They had formed a tight friendship over the last months, forged in torture and death. She wouldn't take things lightly.

With a deep breath, Jackson decided he'd do his damnedest to come back for the express purpose of saving Nora the pain of his loss.

"Hunters," Gustafson yelled, getting the attention of each of the other men in the room, "we've got a trail of attacks to follow to where we believe the target is holed up ... here, in Theo Wirth Park."

Gustafson pointed to a map which had recently been tacked to the wall in the room in which they gathered. He pointed to a few other pins in the map in other parks between the lab's location and the suspected location of Micelli.

"Micelli's been loose for a few hours, and he's moving fast. Whatever the administration of that serum did to him turned him into something wild and rabid. This is a shoot to kill mission. I want him put down as fast as possible with as little fuss as possible. You get a shot, you take it," Gustafson ordered, turning to Jackson with a warning look.

The hard expression on the leader of the Hunter's face said it all: it didn't matter if Jackson thought he should be the one to pull the trigger, it was a matter of public safety to take Micelli down quickly and quietly.

Some of the Hunters around them fidgeted uncomfortably, and it was to them Gustafson addressed his next comments. "Some of you are having some issues coming to terms with taking down a fellow Hunter. I'd be happy to show you the video of what he did to two *Vampire* guards with almost no effort. He's lethal, and from what I've been told by the *other* Vampire doctor, it is highly likely the effects of the serum are irreversible. Anyone got any issues?"

None of the Hunters stepped forward with grievances, so Gustafson ordered them on their way.

"Oh, one more thing," Gustafson called out to the group, stopping them all in their tracks. "Jackson better come back alive. If he doesn't, I'll shoot the first Hunter who walks through that door myself."

Grumbles of dissension and a few mutterings under breath followed the proclamation before Gustafson held up his hand to silence them. "The truth is, none of us know what happened in that bunker. We only know what Rodriguez told us. We all know that fucker was a psychopath. I'm not saying Jackson didn't deserve the beat down you all gave him, but I believe we've got more to gain from keeping him alive than shooting him."

"Sir, why is he being allowed to join the contingent?" one of the wary Hunters questioned.

"Because that was his girl on the table in the other room—a human—her execution ordered by Micelli. If it were you, wouldn't you want your pound of flesh?" Gustafson asked, pointing in the general direction of the lab where Alicia's body lay.

Noises of reluctant assent filtered through the group. Jackson fought valiantly against the rage threatening to consume him, prompting him to break whatever was in his way at the mention of Alicia's death. Deep breaths calmed him so he could file from the room with the others. He'd save his anger for when it was needed when he faced off with Micelli.

"Get going," Gustafson ordered to the Hunters, followed by Jackson, already marching past him through the door.

CHAPTER TWENTY-TWO

Jody wasn't sure how long she stood there, soaking Zeke's shirt with her tears, but not once had he asked her to stop or tried to move away. She was extremely thankful to have his strength when she felt so weak.

The clomping gait of boot-clad Hunters echoed loudly in the halls, and Jody steeled herself for the final good-bye. This was it, they were coming to take Alicia away. Jody moved into the room to gaze down at the serene expression on her sister's face. Frowning down at the body, Jody noticed something had changed.

A great gasp startled Jody and she stumbled backward as Alicia sat up on the table and let out a blood-curdling scream. Hands clasped over her mouth, Jody watched in horror while Alicia's panicked expression took in her surroundings. It was all at once the most terrifying and beautiful sight Jody had ever seen.

"Oh my God," she gasped, reaching for her sister.

Zeke held her back, arms wrapped around her middle. Alicia hadn't stopped screaming, the sounds incoherent and eerie. The footsteps that had echoed through the hallway at a languorous pace earlier could now be heard running toward them.

Drawing up next to Jody, Endre's eyes were riveted on Alicia's hysterical form. Jody didn't bother to turn to look at him, her attention fixed on her sister.

"Shhhh," Endre shushed, scooping Alicia from where she had lain dead only moments earlier. He cradled her against his chest like a child and continued shush her. The screaming quieted and Endre spoke to her in a soothing tone, "That's right, deep breaths in and deep breaths out. You're doing great."

Alicia's eyes were screwed tightly shut, a look of pain distorting her features. Jody longed to hold her like Endre did, to soothe away the agony. She took a step closer when Zeke released her, but Endre held up a hand to ward her off.

"She will need to feed, and likely won't be able to control her cravings. Since you are the only human in the room, you should probably stay back for a few more moments," he warned.

Jody did as he bid, watching helplessly, unable to do anything but observe.

After a few moments, watching the progressive calm take over Alicia, Jody couldn't help but offer some kind of assistance.

"What can I do to help?" Jody asked softly, keeping the table between them.

At the sound of Jody's voice, Alicia's eyes opened and focused on her. They were all at once the familiar eyes of her sister and yet different. The pupils were blown out as if she'd just gotten dilation eye drops. The woman grasping desperately at Endre was her sister in body, Jody just hoped there was still some of Alicia inside.

Overwhelming sound assaulted Alicia's ears—loud thumping heartbeats, the whir of the machines in the lab, the scratching of bugs in the walls. She wanted to cover her ears and drown them all out, all except the soothing shushing of whoever held her. The arms were strong, masculine. But they were the wrong ones. They weren't the arms she wanted around her. Panic started to creep in, not knowing whose arms held her, but knowing they didn't belong to Jackson. She was sure she'd know Jackson's embrace anywhere, and this wasn't it.

A new sound joined the overly loud cacophony, one she recognized and calmed her panic instantly. *Jody.* Alicia's eyes sprang open and she immediately regretted the fervor with which she wanted to see her sister. The light was bright and burned into her retinas, her pupils taking in too much of it at a time. Slowly realization dawned on her, bits and pieces coming together to solve the current puzzle she lived. She tried to push the pieces away, hoping to live in ignorance for a few blissful moments before she was forced to face reality and the situation she found herself in.

When the burn subsided from her eyes, Alicia focused on the figure standing across the room. A facsimile of Jody stood in front of her, but everything about her was all wrong. The small lines around her eyes and mouth were more prominent. The flecks of dark blue in her eyes nearly identical to Alicia's were somehow darker. It looked like Jody, but more detailed.

"Hi Al," Jody breathed out, tears leaving wet trails down her cheeks.

Jody's heartbeat was erratic and the stench of fear permeated the room. Alicia's stomach knotted with anxiety. Jody was afraid of her. Her sister had never been afraid of her before. There was only one reason she'd fear her now. Alicia knew what it was, she just didn't want to name it or think about it. She just wanted to bask in the presence of the sister she thought she'd never see her again.

"Hi Jo," Alicia responded, her voice hoarse from disuse ... or screaming. It was probably the screaming. Waking up when she thought she was dead had been terrifying.

A sob shook Jody, and just as a big sister should, Alicia longed to remove herself from the lap she sat on and comfort her baby sister. Whose lap *was* she on? She was almost afraid to look. But, she was nothing if not curious, so look she did. Turning her head slightly, she caught the sight of blond hair and blue eyes she was convinced loathed her before.

"Endre," she gasped in surprise.

He hated her, why was she on his lap? *Oh God, Nora's going to kill me.*

Endre let out a chuckle before unwinding his arms from her. "*Al*," he acknowledged with a grin. Curious, Alicia could almost swear she saw relief in his expression.

Alicia slid from his lap, not even sure if she could stand on her own, but was careful she didn't accidentally touch anywhere she shouldn't. Her feet landed on the ground and she rose with more grace than she was pretty sure she'd ever possessed in her life. *But then again, this is a new life, isn't it?* The little voice in her head was back again, trying to make her admit things she didn't want to think about—not even with her little voice.

Astonished eyes measured her every move when she stepped closer to Jody. The dude next to her, who Alicia had never seen before, pulled her sister in close in a way that could only be described as protective. Alicia eyed him carefully, taking in the way Jody clung to him in return, the gesture entirely too comfortable for this to be some stranger offering comfort.

"I'm Zeke," the guy offered, answering the unspoken question.

Well, that explained things a little bit. Kind of. They knew each other. But by the looks of the embrace, they also *knew* each other. Alicia frowned at the couple, unsure why the idea of her sister being with a Vampire bothered her so much. Hadn't she been performing the same experimenting with Jackson?

Vampire. *Oh God.* There it was, the little voice just dropped the 'V' word on her like a bomb. It was the only explanation that made sense. The last thing Alicia remembered before waking up screaming like a freaking banshee was being shot. Rubbing her hand over where the bullet had entered her chest, she felt a dull ache there. Would it ever go away? Damn. She was a Vampire. That sucked. Well, she would be *sucking,* she supposed. But at least she could think of a few pros to this—she wasn't dead and things with Jackson might be a little easier now that they were both Vampires. Or, at least they would be Vampires until they took the serum.

The serum. Nora had been injected with the serum. Where was Nora?

Alicia looked around the room. Along with Jackson missing, Nora was notably absent. There were also a half dozen huge dudes she had never seen before. One of them shifted uncomfortably when her gaze landed on him, sending a warm current of air wafting across the room. She drew the scent the air carried into her lungs. It was different from the smell Zeke and Endre had—Vampire smell—and it was different from how Jody smelled as a human. Alicia had no clue who or what these guys were. But she was clearly making them nervous.

"Where's Nora?" she inquired, backing up the train of thought to stop at one of the stations she zoomed past.

"She's resting," Endre conceded, his lips pursed, and dare she perceive a look of concern on his face?

"How's she doing after getting the cure?" Alicia questioned, her voice hopeful.

She may not have spent as much time as Endre on the damned cure, but it was an accomplishment she hoped to not only be proud of, but also make use of in the near future.

"Not great," Endre admitted quietly.

Not great? What does that mean?

"She's very weak and deteriorating quickly," Jody chimed in, her voice wavering.

Jody witnessed pain and death on a daily basis, so seeing her sister so shaken could only mean Nora's condition was dire.

"Can I see her?" Alicia asked, not sure where she should begin … with anything. Her thoughts were jumbled, her body felt weird, and seeing everything in high definition was starting to freak her out quite a bit. "Where's Jackson? And who are those guys? And where are the bad guys? Or are *they* the bad guys?" Questions came tumbling from her mouth, unable to stay where she tried to stack them neatly in her brain.

"Those guys are Vampire Hunters," Endre explained.

Alicia expected at least a little degree of alarm, but he seemed perfectly calm. Maybe it was a ruse?

"That's comforting, says the new Vampire," Alicia grumbled, eyeing the men—Hunters, whatever—warily.

"Jackson is with a contingent of them hunting down Micelli," Endre continued, maintaining an expression of effortless casual.

Alicia wondered if that was part of being a Vampire, or if that was part of being really fucking old. She hoped it was part of being a Vampire, because she could definitely use something with less effort right about now.

"Micelli?" she puzzled, looking around the room like he might jump out from behind one of the larger pieces of equipment. "Bastard."

"Micelli," Endre said with an unmistakable measure of hostility. "I think it would be best if perhaps you got some rest and then we can tell you the rest."

"I'm pretty sure I rested for quite a while," Alicia snorted, looking at the table, unsure how long she had been lying dead, exactly. "Uh, how long was I dead?"

"Over twenty-four hours," Endre answered solemnly.

"Wow. Is that normal?" she queried, her tone clearly shocked.

"No. I've never seen a transition follow death by any longer than three hours," Endre told her, his eyebrows puckered with obvious confusion.

"We thought you were really dead," came Jody's voice from behind Alicia.

She didn't *mean* to ignore her sister, there was just a lot of information to take in. A lot had happened, apparently, in the twenty-four plus hours she'd been dead.

A shudder rolled through her. She had been dead.

"So what happens now?" Alicia questioned, looking around at all the faces gawking at her.

"Now …" Endre said, drawing her gaze back to his face. It was too bad he was such an asshole, the man was h-o-t *hot*. Then again, he was pretty hung up on Nora and Alicia was head over her damned heels for Jackson. "You need to feed on human blood to complete the transition."

"Shit," Alicia breathed out. She'd seen enough blood memories to know feeding was not going to be pretty … or easy.

Everyone in the room turned to look at Jody— the only human among them.

Nope. There was no way she was going to stick her fangs into her baby sister.

"No," Alicia refused, shaking her head to emphasize just exactly *how* emphatic she was about not feeding from her sister. "Aren't there blood bags here or something?"

"There are no blood bags here except your sister," Endre told her.

"Hey," Jody objected, her face twisted in an expression of indignation.

"Can we, like, put the blood in a glass or something? I won't bite her," Alicia protested.

Walking silently toward a row of beakers, Endre plucked one from a stand then returned to Jody, handing it to her with raised eyebrows. Jody looked down at it and then up to Zeke, a silent conversation passing between them. How were they that close they could communicate without words? Jody rolled up her sleeve, exposing the pasty white skin of her forearm—a side effect of living in the frozen tundra of Minnesota. Zeke held out his hand toward Endre, never taking his eyes from Jody's. Endre slapped a pad soaked in alcohol in Zeke's hand and he rubbed it up and down her sister's arm before tossing it with perfect aim into the garbage can across the room. He held out his hand again; this time, a scalpel was slapped into it, just like he was some crazy Vampire surgeon. Maybe he was. Alicia had no freaking idea. Jody's expression was laced with pain when Zeke dragged the scalpel down along the skin of her arm.

Jody's pain momentarily forgotten, Alicia focused her attention on the red welling from the cut and the coppery scent of blood filling the air.

CHAPTER TWENTY-THREE

The frigid wind whipped violently through the trees, the howling sound ripping across pine branches akin to a freight train bearing down on the Hunters in their search for Micelli. The icy tendrils cut through even the warmest clothing, and Jackson had to suppress the urge to shiver to keep warm. Not for the first time, Jackson wondered how the hell people could stand living someplace so cold.

Boots crunched across crisp snow, the sound doing nothing to hide their position or intention. They moved as one cohesive unit, fanned out across an expanse of tree-line park land, stalking toward their prey. Once Jackson had located Micelli by scent, he had to maneuver the team so they approached from downwind. They weren't certain Micelli would be able to smell them, but based on the purely animalistic actions Jackson witnessed in the videos for the lab, he didn't want to take any chances.

A gust blew through, freezing the scant amount of skin exposed on his face, then quiet settled over the park, the only sound the creaking of tree branches from the residual movement of the wind. It was in those moments Jackson would seize the opportunity to take a whiff of the air and hone in on Micelli's location. The scent was stronger; they were on the right track. Jackson held up his hand and silently directed the team to veer slightly to the north. He may no longer be counted among their ranks, but the training of a Hunter never left him.

Breaking branches caught Jackson's ear and he tilted his head to hear it above the raging wind. Something was hurtling through the trees, breaking through substantially sized branches and headed straight for them. In a series of rapid hand movements, Jackson directed the team to take up defensive positions. Micelli knew they were there and was coming to face them head-on.

The Hunters stood frozen, their weapons aimed where Jackson pointed them to. It would have seemed too long of a time to stay idle if he hadn't heard the rapidly approaching enemy. Holding up his hand, Jackson let the Hunters know there was still an imminent threat. Then the sound changed. Micelli changed direction, running parallel to where they stood waiting.

"Fuck," Jackson swore under his breath and took off at a sprint in the direction he heard Micelli's heavy breathing and darting footsteps.

The Hunters behind him shouted, but he paid them no mind. It seemed there *had* been an alteration in Micelli's makeup. He was running faster than Jackson knew a Hunter could typically run, almost faster than what Jackson could keep up with. Almost. He didn't have time to wait for the Hunters to catch up with him and regroup so they could play this game of cat and mouse with Micelli. He had already attacked several people, though the nature of the attacks were deemed animal mauling of some kind. If citizens looking for a calming walk through the park continued to turn up injured, sooner or later someone was bound to come looking for the culprit. Jackson couldn't imagine the reaction of some poor, hapless animal control team sent to capture the elusive animal when they stumbled upon a rabid Hunter. He wasn't about to let that happen.

Every few paces, he gained a few inches on Micelli. The bastard was fast, but Jackson was still faster. A few feet ahead of him, a flash of movement caught his eye. Pushing his protesting muscles to move even swifter, Jackson was determined to catch the bastard before he could evade them yet again. Zeroing in on the movement, he followed every twist and turn and dodge around trees and other obstacles he didn't bother taking the time to identify. With another burst of speed, he was right on Micelli's heels.

Micelli made the mistake of glancing back at Jackson and snapping rabid jaws at him. It slowed his momentum just enough to allow Jackson to reach a hand out and grasp onto the back of his shirt. Micelli stumbled, but continued to attempt to run, even with Jackson holding him. Jackson yanked his arm back, the cloth of Micelli's shirt clutched in his fist. The sudden change in trajectory sent them both tumbling to the ground.

Recovering first, Jackson scrambled to grab ahold of Micelli's leg with a deathly grip. A warning snarl ripped through Micelli, but Jackson held tight and clawed his way toward his enemy. Micelli kicked with his other foot, landing squarely in Jackson's shoulder, but the hit didn't even faze him. There was no way he was letting this fucker get away. While Micelli continued to struggle in Jackson's grip, he made small advances to contain the writhing beast. When at last Jackson could reach, he swung his fist and connected with Micelli's face with a satisfying crunch of bone. The tang of blood flooded the air and Jackson reveled in the bloodlust that battled to be let free. Jackson had every intention of releasing it to ensure Micelli could never harm anyone again.

Red overtook Jackson's vision, a thin veil that did nothing to obscure his view of the enemy—it only served to him permission to give in to the brutality stirring in his veins. Micelli deserved every bit of it, and Jackson was more than happy to unleash it upon him. Using his fists, Jackson subdued Micelli until his body no longer flailed and fought to be free of Jackson's heaving form. With great gasping breaths, Jackson surveyed his handiwork. Micelli's face was nearly unrecognizable, a mass of bloody meat not even fit for the birds to pick at. Rattling breaths still escaped through his mutilated mouth, but Jackson didn't intend to endure the noise much longer.

The pistol aimed squarely in the middle of Micelli's forehead, waiting for Jackson to squeeze the trigger. He didn't hesitate out of some noble sense of guilt or mercy. His avoidance of ending Micelli was borne of malice. He wanted to see the man gasp for air through broken bones and the blood no doubt drowning him from the inside. It was simple … Jackson wanted to revel in his suffering.

Far off shouts roused Jackson from the admiration of his handiwork. It was time to put an end to this. An end to Micelli. It wasn't the extent of suffering Jackson desired, but he feared no matter what he did to Micelli, it would never be enough. Dark eyes filled with hatred stared up at him, daring him to do what was necessary. Jackson was only too happy to oblige. With a squeeze of his finger, Jackson dispatched a monster.

The sound of the gunshot rang like a loud harbinger of finality in Jacksons ears, but the noise was quickly swallowed up in the howling of the wind. Running footsteps and shouts drew the band of Hunters nearer. Jackson stood on heavy legs and faced the direction from which they came. He tucked his pistol in the holster and held his hands up in surrender as they swarmed from the trees and surrounded where he stood over Micelli's corpse.

When the Hunters realized who stood before them and who lay on the ground, most of them lowered their weapons. A few still trained them on Jackson, daring him to gorge on the blood staining the white snow a brilliant red.

"Jesus," one of the Hunters whispered, taking in the unrecognizable state of Micelli's face.

Jackson chanced a look down at his victim, both nauseated and all at once satisfied with what he saw. He took several deep breaths, soothing the beast within back to the depths.

"Take the body and burn it, I don't want to take any chances," Jackson ordered, his eyes fixed on the gruesome sight.

Though it was not his place to issue orders, the Hunters obeyed them. Two scooped up the body of Micelli and carted it off—presumably to the truck in which they arrived at the park. Jackson suspected the body would be brought back to the lab to be incinerated, his ashes left to mingle with his co-conspirators. And Alicia. The thought of even the dust of Micelli left to touch any part of Alicia surged fury through him. It took minutes of deep cleansing breaths of the frozen air to tame the demon within. He would speak to Gustafson—plead with him if he had to—to request Alicia's remains be kept separate from the taint of Micelli and Rodriguez. Jackson just hoped Gustafson would grant him the small act of mercy.

Hunters swarmed around him, theirs scents a mix of apprehension and fear, though their blank expressions hid it well. Two others removed the bloody snow, scooping it into garbage bags and hauling those back to the truck, too.

"It's over," the gladiator told him, breaking into his reverie.

His heavy hand landed on Jackson's shoulder, just as a comrade would congratulate his brother in arms. It took every ounce of control Jackson clung tightly to not to rip the Hunter's arm from his socket, the red having not completely receded from his vision. Several more deep breaths followed until Jackson retained full control over his body and mental faculties. By the end, he was mildly surprised his lungs weren't frozen from the icy air.

The gathered Hunters gave him a few more wary glances before silently moving across the tundra to join the others at the truck. Jackson watched wispy clouds race across the night sky on their way back, falling into thoughts of existential crisis. The cure had been his singular focus for months, until Alicia had stepped into the picture. Then, seeking revenge on her killer had taken its place. Now, he didn't know where he should concentrate his efforts. A niggling voice told him to stay and help reformulate the cure. A louder voice asked him what the point was. He'd wanted the cure to be human—or a Hunter—again so he could have a normal life. But a normal life was never in the cards for him, not having been born a Hunter. Even if the cure could have saved him from the labors of Hunter life, he wasn't sure he wanted to live it without Alicia. He'd pinned so many of his hopes of the future on their short time together, he hadn't even fully realized it. Now that she was gone, he had no idea which direction he should take.

"Let's move out, men," the gladiator ordered, startling Jackson back to where he stood before the truck. Obeying the command, the group of Hunters clamored into the truck.

Jackson climbed into the bed next to where Micelli's body lay on a tarp, his face covered by a corner of it. Jackson was glad for it; he didn't want that face staring up at him while he wandered lost in his own mind. An uncertain future awaited him back at the lab and he didn't know how he was going to find purpose again.

CHAPTER TWENTY-FOUR

Jody's hand shook as she handed the beaker of collected blood to Alicia. She didn't know how wise it was to be handing blood to a new Vampire with an open wound, she just hoped her sister could control herself enough not to attack her.

Alicia cautiously took the glass instrument from her, and promptly took a step back, her gaze riveted on the cut on Jody's arm for a moment, then was transfixed on the gathered blood in her hand. Jody couldn't watch her sister drink, it would just be the final nail in the coffin, so to speak. It wasn't that she didn't know what Alicia was now, but some part of her was still in denial. Or shock. Or both, probably. Turning her back to Alicia, she faced Zeke, who had a matching cut on his arm and was proffering the bloody wound to her.

"You just need a little bit to heal," Zeke prompted, holding up his arm.

"Yay, more blood," Jody murmured, catching the smirk on Zeke's face as she licked at the blood on Zeke's arm. Which was weird.

The satisfied smacking of lips met her ears and Jody couldn't help rolling her eyes. Alicia's lip smacking while eating or drinking anything was undoubtedly Jody's biggest pet peeve, and Alicia knew it. She turned back to her sister, who held the now-empty beaker in her hand. Alicia gave her a smile that showed bloody teeth, the sight making her cringe.

"Gross," Jody commented, disgust blatant in her voice.

Alicia's response was to burst out laughing, as if it was commentary on a burp or a fart. The imagery of childhood air expulsion battles made Jody laugh—not that she would ever admit they did those kinds of things, she was a lady after all. Somehow, in all this she was glad she could laugh. Alicia covered her mouth and ran her tongue over her teeth under her lips.

"Well, I guess I get to know all your secrets now," Alicia declared mischievously, a single eyebrow raised. Jody didn't even know she could do that with her eyebrow.

"Oh God!" Jody gasped out when the realization hit her.

There were going to be some interesting things over the last few days she wasn't exactly thrilled with her sister seeing in the blood memory things … like her time with Zeke, or the numerous times Rodriguez threatened or attempted to rape her.

"If you could just, you know, skip over the last couple of days and ignore anything with Zeke in it, that would be great," Jody groaned, covering her face with her miraculously healed forearm. Now she just had to make sure she didn't die so it wouldn't be her drinking blood from a beaker and smiling with gruesome red teeth.

"You both seem to have a surprising sense of humor about all this," Endre observed, his voice cutting sharp across the horrific thoughts running through Jody's head.

"I think this is one of those situations where if you don't laugh, you're definitely going to cry," Alicia offered, her lower lip wobbling like she might be ready to indulge in the latter.

Jody moved forward to pull Alicia into a hug, just like she wanted to ever since she came back to life. Zeke's hand on her shoulder stopped her and she glanced nervously at her sister.

"Can I hug you, or are you going to try to eat me?" Jody eyed her sister suspiciously.

"Um, I think I should be okay?" Alicia debated, biting her lip and looking to Endre for confirmation.

"We'll be right here if something happens," Zeke assured, standing so close he was almost touching her.

"Yeah, Endre's just over there wishing for me to do something stupid so he can hit me or something." Alicia glanced over to where the brooding Vampire stood.

A smirk lifted half Endre's mouth, so close to an actual smile Jody couldn't help but chuckle herself.

Pulling Alicia into the circle of her arms, Jody gave her what would have been a crushing hug, but she suspected as a Vampire it did less harm than it used to.

Alicia rested her cheek on Jody's shoulder and let out a sigh.

"We'll figure this out," Jody reassured. "We'll get your cure figured out."

Alicia nodded, her cheek rubbing against Jody's shoulder and her hair tickling her cheek.

"Can I go see Nora now?" Alicia's voice came softly.

"I'll see if she's awake," Endre said, leaving the room.

The Hunters loomed in the doorway, shooting nervous glances in their direction. Jody was fairly certain they were more used to the philosophy that 'the only good Vampire is a dead Vampire'. They simply didn't know what to do with themselves when they weren't taking well-aimed shots at their enemies.

"Are they just going to watch us?" Alicia mumbled into her shoulder, as if plucking the thought from Jody's head.

"Probably. I don't think they know what to do when they're not killing a Vampire on sight," Jody answered dryly.

It was strange, going from fearing the very idea of Vampires just a few days ago to having two in her life she would protect to her last breath if she had to. She supposed it would be three if she counted Nora, and she did. Endre she was still on the fence about, he was a cantankerous SOB, but she figured he couldn't be *all* bad if Nora loved him. Then there was Jackson, who she could see plain as day was devastated at the loss of

Alicia when they thought her dead. That alone put him into her "Vampires to trust" category.

"Jackson doesn't know you came back," Jody whispered.

Alicia snorted. "That's going to be a bit of a shocker."

"Al, he was absolutely *devastated* when he saw you lying on that table. I don't think I've ever seen a more broken man." Jody pulled her away so she could fully convey the true gravity of what she said.

"Really?" Alicia asked, sniffling. Tears leaked from the corners of her eyes.

"Really," Jody reiterated, pulling Alicia into another tight hug. She couldn't believe less than a half hour ago she thought she was going to watch her sister's body burn.

"What happened to Jackie?" Alicia inquired suddenly, pulling out of her embrace and looking up at Jody with big, terrified eyes.

Zeke let out a loud exhale behind her and Jody had to take a few moments to gather her thoughts on how she was going to explain it all to Alicia. Jackie had been Alicia's friend, Jody didn't know how Alicia was going to take her ultimate betrayal and eventual death. How would she react when she learned her *friend* was the ultimate cause of all this misery?

"Do you want the long version or the short version?" Jody queried carefully.

Alicia's brows pinched together in confusion and maybe even a little concern. "I think maybe my brain will only be able to take the short version." The resigned look in Alicia's eyes told Jody she already knew the final outcome.

"Okay," Jody started, leading them over to a pair of stools tucked under the edge of a workbench. "Jackie wasn't really Jackie, she was *Jaqueline*. She was a Vampire." Alicia gasped, but didn't interrupt. "Turns out Endre saved her life by turning her into a Vampire a few centuries ago, and she had been in love with him the whole time. She tricked Micelli into helping her get Endre dug up from his grave, or whatever, so she could swoop in and tell him it was her that saved him. But then Nora happened, and Jaqueline lost track of them. So, her mission went from rescue to revenge. She was the one who got the Hunters to kidnap Nora."

"And tortured," Endre interjected as he entered the room, cradling Nora in his arms. "By Rodriguez. But I think this is a good time to put a hold on the rest of your story."

"Oh, Nora," Alicia gasped, hand over her mouth. Jody didn't know if she was upset over the idea of Rodriguez torturing Nora or the sight of Nora's emaciated form.

Alicia rushed over to where Endre held Nora, Jody following quickly behind.

"Have we figured out what's wrong?" Jody questioned Endre with sad eyes.

Nora looked even worse off than the last time Jody had laid eyes on her. Her body seemed to have shrunken, her skin sallow and baggy, almost like her body was devouring her from the inside. A moment of inspiration hit Jody. Maybe her body *was* eating her from the inside.

"Nora, are you hungry?" Jody inquired gently, petting the woman's dark hair.

Endre glared at Jody, as if he thought she was taunting them. He brushed past Jody and ever so carefully placed Nora's frail body on the table Alicia had been revived from not so long ago.

"Just listen for a second. Look at her. If you were evaluating her as a physician, what would you see?" Jody challenged, placing her fingers on Nora's wrist to count her pulse.

It was almost as if a light literally went on in Endre's head. His eyes lit up with purpose and he turned to the Hunters gathered at the door.

"Go get some food!" Endre shouted at them.

They looked at each other nervously, but none of them made any indication of following Endre's brusque order.

Jody turned to Zeke, pleading with her eyes.

Giving her a reassuring smile, he put a hand on her shoulder. "What should I get?" he asked, taking on her unspoken plea without complaint.

"Let's start off simple. We're just going to have to see what works. Get some meal replacement shakes. Not the dieting kind, something like Ensure. Get Pediasure if you can't find the adult variety. Also, grab some protein powder, some kind of electrolyte replacing drink, and multi-vitamins. See if you can find something liquid, nothing she'd have to swallow whole," Jody listed off to Zeke, ticking each thing off on her fingers while she compiled a list. "Do you need me to write this down?"

Zeke tapped his temple and gave her a wink. "It's all up here."

"Thank you," Jody breathed, looking up at Zeke like the knight in shining armor he was.

She didn't know how the Hunters could fail to see the goodness in Vampires like him. A shudder ran through her at the thought of him encountering their 'shoot first, don't bother asking questions' mentality.

"You okay?" He rubbed his hands up and down her arms, chasing away the quaking of her body.

She plastered on a smile. "Yeah."

"All right, I'll be back as soon as I can." Zeke pressed his lips lightly to hers before leaving.

"Wow," Alicia breathed, bringing Jody's attention from the doorway devoid of Zeke.

"What?" Jody asked, busying herself with checking Nora's vitals.

"You've got it bad," Alicia stated, examining her from head to toe.

Jody wasn't going to deny it. It was absolutely true. Her only response was a sheepish smile. Alicia shook her head with a smirk, but turned her attention to Nora when a small groan escaped her. She was deteriorating quickly and Jody just hoped by the time

Zeke came back with some nourishment there wasn't irreparable damaged.

CHAPTER TWENTY-FIVE

"Lamb, is there anything I can get you?" Endre asked in a soothing voice while he pet her hair.

He was unaccustomed to feeling so helpless, so useless. Nora's eyes fluttered open briefly, the green in them dull and listless. She was hardly coherent anymore, her mental faculties deteriorating right along with her body. She'd taken some of Zeke's blood during the battle with Rodriguez, but similar to a drug-induced high, she crashed right after the relief the blood provided was spent.

"Do you think we should try more Vampire blood?" Jody questioned uncertainly.

Endre had to admit, though he wasn't terribly fond of her sister, Jody's attentiveness to Nora earned his respect. The woman was an excellent nurse, keeping a relatively calm head even with the sights of blood and gore she'd witnessed over the last several days.

"It might help until Zeke returns," Endre admitted.

"Should I give her mine?" Alicia offered, watching Endre roll his sleeve up. He could see the guilt swimming in her unshed tears.

Endre glowered back at her, cutting across his wrist with his fangs while holding her shamed gaze. If Nora was to get anyone's blood, it would be his. He dribbled blood into Nora's open mouth, watching the fragile curve of her throat as she swallowed. When he turned his angry gaze back to Alicia, she hung her head, contrite.

At least the new Vampire understood Nora's rapid decline was as a result of her hastily formulated cure. He wanted to fault Alicia for what happened to Nora, needing someone to blame, but he knew it wasn't entirely her doing. The cure had not been perfect, but Alicia *had* done her due diligence and intended to test the cure out on her captured aggressor before it was administered to any of them. In the end, it wasn't Alicia's fault Nora had been injected with the ill-tested serum. In the end, the culprits to blame for his love's current state were all ashes in the incinerator downstairs. All except Micelli, who Endre was confident Jackson would be taking great pains to remedy.

Nora's heartbeats grew stronger and her breaths deeper with the temporary infusion of blood. Endre just hoped Jody's theory of starvation was correct. It seemed to make sense that a body subsisting solely off blood for months would harvest nutrients from itself once that supply was depleted. In reality, it wasn't that different from when he had been buried and starved, his body fed off his tissues and desiccated as a means of survival. The difference here, however, was as far as they knew, Nora was no longer immortal and Endre had no desire to test the theory by allowing her heart to cease beating. Their only hope was to get some human nutrition into her mostly-human body now.

Alicia paced nervously while they awaited Zeke's return. Watching Nora's body waste away was horrifying, especially knowing the serum she'd concocted was the cause. What was even more gut-wrenching was the fact she had nothing to do to help while they waited. Zeke had only been gone for twenty minutes or so, and Jody had concluded the "short" version of what had transpired while Alicia had been dead. There had been so much death and carnage over one deranged woman's obsession. A part of her felt like she should have known something was off about Jackie, but the other part reminded her that Jackie had played the part of her friend perfectly. It wasn't as though she had known Vampires were even a real thing until a week ago.

The roar of an engine *outside* halted Alicia's unsettled pacing. She didn't know if she would ever get used to being able to hear things so far away and through several layers of brick. Right now, she could hear the Hunters jogging through the hallway to the back door. A lot of Hunters. Nervousness swept through her. Was it Zeke returned from his grocery run, or Jackson back from his revenge mission?

More movement throughout the building continued to draw her attention in every direction. There were quite a few people moving around in their little sanctuary. It was strange after having spent several days here before her death where the place was silent as a tomb.

Zeke's voice echoed down the hall, addressing the Hunters with neither hostility nor friendliness. Alicia had to admit she was disappointed it wasn't Jackson coming toward them, but the sight of Zeke with bags of nourishment for Nora was more than welcome—even if it wasn't what she was anxious to see.

"Where can I put these?" he asked, holding up a paper bag in each hand.

"Uhhh," Jody debated, scrambling to open the fridge in the lab and finding it full of chemicals and specimens. "We'll have to put it in the fridge out here," she told him reluctantly and directed Zeke toward the little break room adjacent to the lab.

Alicia watched their exchange, both jealous and fascinated. She hadn't thought she'd miss Jackson as much as she did, but watching her sister with her new beau stirred up a longing for Jackson's strong arms to comfort her and take away the horrors of the last twenty-four hours, if even for a few moments. She'd never seen Jody like this with a guy before. She'd never really seen Jody with a guy before at all. Her sister worked long, erratic hours at the hospital and claimed not only was it hard to fit in the time to meet someone, but it was also difficult to find a someone who was understanding enough to handle the crazy hours she dedicated to her job. On the flip side, Alicia worked a normal nine to five type job and hadn't been able to find a guy interested in her until she met Jackson. At least she could say something positive came out of the last week.

"Don't you dare touch any of that food," Alicia heard Jody warning the Hunters gathered in the small kitchenette. "If you want food, go get your own damned food."

Zeke stifled a laugh and Alicia couldn't help the smile that crossed her face. Leave it to Jody to threaten men who could break her in half with no effort at all.

"What's this?" Jody questioned, confusion evident in her voice.

"I thought you might want some food of your own," Zeke's deep rumble responded.

"Thank you," Jody whispered.

It was official, Alicia liked Zeke. He was taking care of her sister, he could stay.

"Eavesdropping isn't very polite," Nora admonished, smirking at her from where she lay on the table.

"Oh shut up," Alicia mumbled, but couldn't contain her smile. "They're just so cute."

Nora laughed.

"Is there anything I can get you?" Alicia asked earnestly. She wanted to do something to help. Badly. The idle pacing and worrying were driving her insane.

"I think Jody's got it covered, she's more of a hoverer than you," Nora chuckled as she nodded to where Jody and Zeke approached from the door. Alicia was glad to see Nora had regained enough strength to speak again.

"Which flavor?" Jody offered, holding up a bottle in each hand. "We have vanilla and chocolate here, and there's strawberry in the fridge."

Nora wrinkled her nose in distaste at the sight of the nutrition shakes.

"I doubt it tastes any worse than blood," Jody chided. That earned a laugh from Endre.

Alicia looked at him in amazement. She'd never seen the man smile, let alone *laugh*. She had most definitely woken up in an alternate universe.

"What's it going to be?" Jody demanded, giving Nora a no-nonsense look Alicia could imagine she used with her most difficult patients.

"Fine," Nora grumbled sourly, "I'll try the vanilla."

"Good." Jody twisted open the bottle. "Here you go," she offered, handing what was probably an absolutely disgusting meal over to Nora.

Nora wrinkled her nose again as she sniffed the shake. "This smells gross."

Alicia had to agree, she could smell it from where she stood, and it smelled so medicinal to her nose, it overpowered the vanilla aroma that was meant to make it appealing enough to choke down.

"Nora," Jody warned, propping her free hand on her hip.

Endre chuckled again, the sound odd in Alicia's ears. She silently watched the battle of wills between Jody and Nora, coming to the impression the two must have spent some time together over the last day. They seemed familiar and comfortable with one another.

Nora raised the bottle to her lips and took a swallow. "Oh, that is god-awful," she choked with a grimace.

Jody tried to hide her smile, but failed miserably.

"You're enjoying this, aren't you?" Nora accused Jody.

"I just want to see you get healthy," Jody told her sincerely, all traces of humor dropping from her face.

"I know." A sad smile crossed her face.

"Drink half and then you'll need to take the other half in sixty minutes," Jody ordered, looking up at the clock on the wall.

While Jody strode over to the bench and set an alarm on one of the timers there, Nora gulped down the ordered amount of the shake, all the while grimacing.

"Here, to wash out the taste," Zeke said, offering a bottle of red Gatorade.

Nora took the bottle and gulped from it gratefully.

"Not too much!" Jody warned, rushing back over to the table.

When half that bottle was gone, she handed it back to Zeke with a grateful, "Thanks."

Alicia pegged him as a man of few words; he was quiet and observant, his gaze following Jody's movements with careful observation. He offered comfort without her request and steadied her when she stumbled.

"It's time for you to eat now," Zeke admonished Jody.

"I agree," Alicia chimed in, feeling almost as if her presence in the room had been forgotten.

It was a foreign feeling, watching her sister take charge where she normally would have.

"I think you should shower and change," Jody shot back, pointedly looking at Alicia's blood-stained clothing.

Alicia glanced down at herself. She could definitely use a shower and fresh clothes. The shirt she wore still sported a hole where the bullet plunged into her chest cavity and ended her life.

"I think everyone could use some freshening up," Endre acknowledged, rising to his feet. "Let's meet back here in an hour for Nora's next feeding. We'll assess progress and begin to run some tests to determine the best course of action to take for reformulation of the cure."

Every head in the room nodded with weary assent. Alicia had a feeling she was in for a long night. Or day. She didn't even have a clue what day or time of day it was.

Alicia's feet automatically took her to Jackson's room. It was like instinct was driving her to be nearer to where she could smell him. His quarters also smelled like blood and bleach—the bleach doing more to clean up the stains than to drown out the scent. Faint traces of Jody and Nora also permeated the room, and it wasn't hard to decipher this was where they were held captive by Jackie. *Jaqueline.*

What horrors had they endured while she was dead? Alicia supposed she'd end up seeing some of it when Jody's blood memories took over her sleep. It was inevitable, just like the idea she was a Vampire now, but that didn't mean she had to be happy with it. In her mind, it was also just as inevitable she would cure herself and not remain a full Vampire any longer. If her initial assessments of Nora were any indication, it seemed no cure she could formulate would make her wholly human again.

With a deep sigh of resignation for her new lot in life, Alicia pulled clean scrubs from Jackson's dresser and made her way to the bathroom. She could shed tears for her changed life in the privacy of the water.

CHAPTER TWENTY-SIX

Zeke watched like a hawk while she scarfed down a yogurt and then moved on to a banana. Jody had to remind herself to take it slow. She may not be as starved as Nora, but she'd still gone quite a while without food. If she binged, she'd just see it all coming back up in a matter of minutes.

"How are you doing?" Zeke inquired, and Jody had a feeling he wasn't talking about her hunger.

"I think everything is still sinking in," Jody answered around a mouthful of banana. Zeke didn't even flinch at her lack of manners.

"And your sister?" Zeke pried.

"I don't care what she is, as long as she's alive," Jody admitted after adopting some better manners and swallowing her mouthful of food. "Besides," she shrugged, "she'll continue to work on the cure. If there's anything about my sister you should know, it's that she's relentless."

Zeke nodded, but Jody knew he could see right through her. She was terrified. Terrified Alicia wouldn't be *Alicia* anymore after her transition. Terrified Alicia wouldn't be able to formulate a cure that wouldn't desiccate them all.

"She'll figure it out," Zeke agreed. Standing, he threw her banana peel in the garbage and dumped her spoon and yogurt cup into the sink.

How he knew yogurt was one of her most favorite foods, she had no idea. Maybe he'd guessed. Either way, there absolutely was swooning when she'd seen he'd not only brought back food for Nora, but picked up things for her, too. Jody had almost forgotten the timespan since her last meal when he'd left, her hunger pangs so far gone they didn't register anymore.

Looking up at the clock, Zeke squinted at it. "There are still forty-five minutes until everyone reconvenes in the lab. Did you want a shower before we go back?"

"God yes," Jody groaned. "I could use some company," she suggested playfully.

Heat flared in his eyes as he stalked toward her. She'd take that as acceptance of her invitation. Strong hands lifted her to her feet. Zeke's lips were on hers in an instant, treating her to a demanding kiss. Jody needed to get him naked and in the bathroom, stat.

"Everyone will hear us," Zeke warned against her lips, but didn't stop kissing her.

"I don't even care right now."

She *needed* this. She needed to take her mind off everything and she could see no better way to do that than to replace her thoughts with sensation.

A rush of air left her lungs as Zeke whisked her up into his arms, in search of the nearest shower. Jody hadn't the faintest idea where to go, but Zeke seemed to know because he followed the twisting corridors until he came to an unoccupied bathroom. They didn't bother to look for towels or clean clothing to change into, the only thoughts occupying Jody's mind were of just how good Zeke would feel naked and wet under her hands.

Not breaking stride, or the connection of their lips, Zeke flicked on the light and kicked the door shut behind them. When he set her on the floor, they tugged at each other's clothing, laying one another bare within seconds.

The sight of Zeke naked and already hard for her caught Jody's breath in her throat. He was equally enamored of the view of her skin before him. She watched his eyes rove over her, her skin growing warm with his appraisal, despite the chill in the air.

He stalked slowly toward her, need and hunger burning in his eyes. His mouth was set in a playful smirk that sent her heart aflutter. Jody took a step backward, and then another until her back pressed against the wall. A gasp left her when her skin made contact with the frigid tile. Zeke's warm body caged her against the wall, chasing away the cold with nothing but the heat radiating off his skin.

Jody couldn't stand it, being so near without their bodies touching. She *needed* him to touch her, to kiss her, to bury himself deep inside of her. She tentatively ran hands up the lean muscles over his stomach and abs, shivering with delight when he did the same. Tilting her chin toward him, Jody invited him to take her lips in another demanding kiss, and he happily obliged. His mouth came crashing down on hers, the force bruising and edged with a delicious sense of desperation. Large hands cupped her ass and hoisted her so her molten center pressed against the hardness ready for her. Tilting her hips, she encouraged him to slip inside. Zeke held her firm, kneading the flesh of her behind while he continued to attack her mouth, Jody reveling in the passion of each nip and suck.

Frustrated with the lack of penetration, she reached between their bodies, brushing her fingers along the crown of his cock. She longed to grasp it and feel the steely girth against her palm, but Zeke pulled her hand away and pinned it above her head. The feeling of being immobilized by his strong arms sent a surge of anxiety through her. At the erratic change in her heartbeat, Zeke paused his amorous kisses and peered into her eyes, such concern in his gaze.

"You all right?" he rasped, voice thick with need.

Jody looked up at where his hand held her wrist and swallowed. She didn't want to tell him being restrained by him frightened her—because it wasn't that she ever thought he would hurt her, it was more the pain of not being able to touch him that got to her. Zeke followed her gaze and instead of holding her wrist, linked their hands together. It seemed she didn't have to offer an explanation; if he felt she was the least bit uncomfortable, he would rectify the issue.

"Better?" he questioned, a comforting smile on his face.

"Better. Now kiss me."

Zeke was only too happy to oblige. Lips brushed against hers in soft caresses; they were in juxtaposition with the demanding and devouring kisses he lavished her with earlier. He slipped his hand from where their fingers intertwined and deftly reached into the shower to switch on the water. The rushing wave of water reminded Jody there was another purpose to their visit to the bathroom. But she wasn't ready to get clean just yet. Taking advantage of her hand free of Zeke's, she reached again between them, this time grasping his erection in her palm. A long, low moan rumbled through his chest, emboldening Jody. With slow strokes, she wrung animalistic noises and heavy breaths from the Vampire she literally held in her palm.

"Jody," he groaned, burying his face in the crook of her neck.

His hand covered hers to freeze the movement giving him pleasure.

"Slow down, princess," he gasped into her neck. "I won't last if you keep that up."

Jody couldn't help the mischievous grin turning up the corners of her mouth, not that Zeke could see her. She tried to move her hands again, but he held her firm. He pulled his face from where it was buried and confronted her and the Cheshire cat smile on her face.

"That's how you want to play this? I don't think so," he challenged.

The look on his face told her he knew it was all a ploy so he would give her what she wanted. With one swift movement, he lifted her and plunged in right where she needed him. They groaned in harmonized pleasure at the reuniting of their bodies.

"Fuck," Zeke breathed into Jody's hair, blowing the strands to tickle along her neck. "I thought I was never going to see you again." He nipped at her ear.

"I thought you were dead," Jody replied, choking on the words as they came out. She would *not* cry during sex. She wouldn't. "No more talking." She pulled his face to hers, silencing any protests he may come up with by pressing her lips to his.

Zeke thrust with measured strokes, setting her up for a slow-building but what would undoubtedly be a cataclysmic orgasm. She could already feel it, and neither of them had even touched anywhere near her clit. Each thrust was angled perfectly to drag along the perfect spot. It seemed Zeke wasn't going to leave her climax up to chance though. Working his hand between them, he brushed light fingers along the over-sensitized bundle of nerves, all the while continuing to thrust at the torturously good slow pace. She could see there were distinct advantages to having a partner who was ridiculously strong … namely the acrobatics she wasn't sure would be able to be achieved with a being of lesser strength.

Jody leaned her head back against the wall, the chilled ceramic doing nothing to cool the flames Zeke continued to stroke into a full-fledged inferno. All thought abandoned her and she was left with nothing but sensation. She was consumed by the pull of Zeke moving in and out of her, the feeling of his fingers applying exactly the right pressure in exactly the right place. It would only take a few more strokes of those clever digits to send her over the edge. One. Two. Three. Jody's eyes rolled back and she let out a silent scream of pure, unadulterated ecstasy. Dear lord this man knew how to play her body just right.

Demanding lips crashed down on hers, pulling lips between teeth though he didn't bite down. Zeke's tongue demanded entry to her mouth, and had Jody wanted to protest, she didn't think she would have had the strength to. Her climax sucked every ounce of energy from her and she couldn't have been happier. A brush of fingers against her sensitive flesh made her entire body twitch and she could feel Zeke smile against her lips.

It wasn't until Zeke lowered her to the ground on shaky legs she realized he was still hard and unfulfilled.

"What do you want?" Jody offered, ready to drop to her knees in the pursuit of giving him even an ounce of the pleasure he'd given her.

"I already got what I wanted. I watched you come," Zeke assured, keeping hold of her arm to prevent her from kneeling.

"Are you for real?" she questioned incredulously.

That was not going to fly with her. She *always* gave as good as she got, if not better. There was no way she was going to leave her man satisfied. She liked the sound of that—*her man.*

"That doesn't exactly work for me," Jody protested, grabbing onto his still-erect cock.

Zeke's eyebrows jumped in surprise, but he didn't protest. Watching his expression to figure out which touches got the best reactions from him, Jody explored his manhood. She'd never thought too much about penises before, merely considered them a tool for reproduction and sometimes pleasure. Most of her experience with them in the recent past was more of the clinical variety than the pleasurable. But now, she was enraptured just watching the expressions she could evoke with a squeeze or a stroke of Zeke's cock. It was a heady feeling realizing she had the power to put that expression of bliss on a man's face with only her hands.

A shiver ran through Jody when Zeke cupped her breast in his big hand, his fingers kneading into the flesh in a way that sent tingles straight to her sex. She was starting to think it might not be such a bad thing Zeke hadn't come, considering she was ready for another round herself. Jody took her hand from him and stepped away, despite his insistent growl. She slipped between him and the wall while he watched her with narrow eyes filled with lusty demands. Instead of words to reassure him she wasn't going to be leaving him with what she could imagine would be a pretty awful case of blue balls, she turned to face the toilet, bent over, and placed her hands on the seat ... presenting him with an open view of what she offered.

The growl that issued from Zeke was all heat and animal need, the sound so purely carnal, it sent a flutter through Jody's center. Not wasting any time, Zeke grabbed ahold of her hips with both hands and buried himself in her heat. The pace was no longer the languorous tempo where Zeke sought to give her pleasure. It was frantic and needy. It was Zeke taking what he wanted.

Animalistic noises escaped them. There were no tender kisses. There was no talk of fears. There was only ardent coupling. This was purely fucking. The raw need in Zeke's fervent strokes pooled heat between Jody's legs, the need to release the pressure dire.

Balancing on one hand, Jody stroked feverishly between her legs, chasing the climax taunting her right on the edge of the precipice. She squeezed her eyes shut, white stars bursting behind her eyelids. Then she was crashing over the ledge amidst the sounds of a great roar from Zeke as he emptied inside of her. He held her hips tightly and she was grateful for his strength keeping her upright. Wrapping his arms around her, he held her back to his chest where she could feel his heart pounding. Gentle kisses trailed up her neck and over her shoulders while the last pulses of his release faded, each brush of his lips sending a little tingle over her skin.

Without a word, Zeke lifted Jody into the shower she was pretty sure was cold by now. She felt guilty for possibly using up the entire building's supply of hot water, but not nearly guilty enough to regret what she was doing while all that hot water was wasted.

Lukewarm water sprayed down on them, but at least it wasn't freezing like Jody had expected. Besides, she didn't think even with freezing water her body would ever cool down with the way Zeke's hands roamed over her skin, memorizing each dip and curve and imperfection. Jody lathered her hands and did the same, tracing over the definition of muscles beneath taut skin.

When the rest of the hot water ran out and all that remained was cold, no matter how far they turned the knob for hot, they made the mutual decision to conclude their shower. They rubbed water droplets away from one another's skin with threadbare towels, and Jody just could not keep her hands off Zeke. This had never happened to her before. She'd always kind of liked the guys she'd dated—maybe even thought she'd fallen in love a few times—but this was something else. This was powerful. This was crazy. She was pretty sure this was the definition of passion, and she had to admit she was loving every minute of it.

A loud knock sounded at the door, and Jody gave Zeke a panicked look. She knew the Vampires in the building would hear them, but she didn't realize how embarrassed she would be in the aftermath. Thoughts bombarded her, questions running into each other without answers. Had she screamed when she had that last orgasm? She was pretty sure she had. Now they would all know she was a screamer. But what did it matter, really?

It's merely a testament to how phenomenal of a lover Zeke is. There's no reason to be embarrassed. She could tell herself that all she wanted, but she was pretty sure her face would be a permanent shade of scarlet when she walked back into that lab.

"Yeah?" Zeke asked casually, like the entire building of supernatural creatures hadn't just heard them fucking.

"Here," Endre's gruff voice answered, obviously prompting them to open the door.

Zeke wrapped a towel around Jody and pushed her behind him while he wound a towel around his waist. They'd definitely forgotten to grab clean things to wear when they rushed to 'take their shower.' Jody had a feeling that was going to be their new code phrase. If not, she was definitely going to *make* it their code for sneaking off together.

Endre thrust something through the crack in the door Zeke allowed and then was gone. When Zeke showed her the pile of scrubs Endre had tossed at him, Jody couldn't help giggling. At least they weren't the only ones who figured out they were too engrossed in the idea of getting one another naked they forgot about what they were going to put on *after* they got clean.

They dressed quickly in their new clothes and hurried back to the lab, assuming—correctly—they were late for their rendezvous with the group. Jody prepared an apology on their way down the hallway, but wondered what good it would do. When they walked through the doors, Endre and Nora were there, but Alicia was missing.

CHAPTER TWENTY-SEVEN

Jackson watched a couple of the Hunters haul Micelli's limp body into the lab. He'd sat next to the already rotting corpse the entire ride in the back of the truck, smelling the decay setting in. There was no doubt Micelli was really dead, but he wanted to make abso-fucking-lutely sure. He wanted to see him turned to ash. He imagined there were others at the lab who also would like to see the flesh seared from Micelli's bones. At least in theory. He *didn't* imagine it was a pretty sight he could stomach for long. Especially the smell. The smell was going to be horrible for anyone with advanced olfactory senses.

Gustafson met him at the door, his expression full of exhaustion. There was also something else there … relief. Jackson could imagine this fiasco with Micelli had been just as trying on the Hunters as it had been on the Vampires. And now it was over. Or mostly over. They still had to meet the Hunters' demands for the cure, *then* they would be free to live out their lives however they wanted. Jackson imagined he'd likely split from the group, maybe head west. If Jody hadn't had Zeke, he would have wanted to stay to watch out for her, but now not even that would keep him tethered here.

"Nice work, Jackson. Although, I think you scared the shit out of some of the guys," Gustafson lauded, watching the Hunters carry the body down to the incinerator.

"I think there are a few people who would like to watch that body burn," Jackson responded.

Gustafson nodded. "We'll hold off until you've gathered everyone. I can understand the desire to see him burned to ashes."

Without another word, Jackson made his way in the direction he could hear Endre and Nora's voices—the lab.

"You're back!" Nora exclaimed from where she sat on one of the tables.

"We got him. The Hunters have the body downstairs, they're going to throw it in the incinerator if anyone wants to watch," Jackson told them flatly.

"I think maybe you should clean up first," Endre pointed out, looking at Jackson's blood-stained clothing dourly.

"I just want to get this over with," Jackson countered.

"I really think you should go change," Nora suggested.

Jackson glowered at her. It wasn't like Nora to push him. He found he didn't exactly like it.

"I'm going to the basement," he barked at them. "You can come with, or not. I don't really fucking care."

"Jackson," Nora called softly when he turned his back. He honestly *didn't* care what argument she gave, he was going to see this to the end.

Several pairs of footsteps followed Jackson from the room and down the hall. He didn't bother to look to see who came, he knew they all would. They all needed the closure just like he did. He'd felt like a shadow had been following them, haunting them for months, and little did he know at the time that his delusions about being watched had been real. He needed to see it end. Then and only then was he free to go his own way.

Footsteps scuffing down the concrete steps echoed in the mechanical room of the former hospital, the sound too loud for their solemn celebration of freedom. More than a dozen Hunters met them at the bottom of the stairs and Jackson heard the hesitation in his friends' strides. He knew what they were thinking— they were in a room full of men who had trained their whole lives to kill Vampires. Even he had to admit the situation ratcheted up his anxiety. But the Hunters weren't going to kill them before they got their cure, so at least they had that leverage, no matter how small it seemed. It would at least buy them some time. Jackson didn't know how long it would take to work out the kinks in the serum, especially with the ashes of its creator being the only thing left of her.

With a nod to Gustafson, Jackson oversaw Micelli's body being shoved into the gaping steel maw of what would ultimately be his tomb. Light footfalls through the hall in the floor above caught Jackson's attention, distracting him from Micelli's body. The gait was just *wrong*. It was too feminine in a building full of over-muscled men, and all the females he knew to be in the building were next to him. He looked at the group surrounding him, wondering if anyone else heard it. Nora cocked her head with her ear toward the stairs, listening for what Jackson assumed was the same sound. At least he wasn't going crazy. Or at least he wasn't the only one. The footsteps grew more hurried and scrambled down the stairs.

"Did I miss it?" a frantic female voice called.

Jackson's heart stopped. Maybe he was going crazy. He'd heard grief could do that to a person. Her scent hit him before he saw her. It was altered, yet unmistakable. The entire room was silent, or else Jackson didn't hear anything anyone said. His focus was entirely on the figure descending the stairs, revealing her one agonizing inch at a time. When he could finally see her face, he collapsed to his knees in shock.

"Alicia?" he croaked out around the thickness in his throat.

Alicia stopped on the bottom stairs. Biting her lip, she wrung her hands as if nervous to see him.

"Surprise?" she offered hesitantly, her heart beating even faster than his was.

"How? How is this possible?" Jackson questioned, his mouth agape with amazement.

She shook her head uncertainly. "We don't know."

"I'm not hallucinating, am I? I haven't finally lost it, right?" he asked the entire room, still in disbelief. He didn't think he could handle it if she were only an illusion there to haunt him.

"You're not hallucinating, she's alive," Endre interjected.

Jackson wasn't the only one who saw her. But seeing her wasn't enough. He clambered gracelessly to his feet. He needed to touch her. He needed to hold her. Stumbling on numb limbs, he closed the few feet separating them. Alicia didn't move a muscle, seemingly frozen in place. When Jackson could finally reach out and touch her, he started by taking her hands between his. They were warm and the feel of them beneath his fingers nearly broke him.

"Oh God, I missed you," Jackson groaned, running his hands up to cup her downturned face.

She continued to stare at the floor, her heart palpitating. *Why won't she look at me? Doesn't she want to see me?* He tilted her face up to gaze into those blue eyes he thought he'd never see again. They shone glassy with tears; he just hoped they were happy tears.

"I'm a Vampire," she lamented, her bottom lip quivering with the threat of a sob.

"I don't care. I love you. I want you if you're human, Vampire, whatever. I love you," Jackson professed.

He hadn't meant to say it. It seemed too soon for a declaration so bold after knowing one another so little time, but he couldn't help how he felt. This was *definitely* a 'when you know you know' situation. He hadn't gotten to say it before she died, and he wasn't going to make that mistake again now that she'd come back to him.

"You love me?" she questioned in disbelief.

"I hope that's okay," Jackson said, trying to control the stab of disappointment in his chest when she hadn't returned the sentiment.

"That's more than okay. I feel the same way. I just didn't want to tell you that, you know, before because I didn't want to sound like one of those crazy women who latch onto a guy who doesn't want them," she rambled anxiously.

Jackson silenced her nervousness by pressing his lips to hers. The rigid posture of her body melted away and he caught her up in his arms before she slid to the floor.

"I love you, too," she whispered when he finally let her come up for air.

A cheer sounded from the audience they forgot they had. Alicia hid her face in his chest, an embarrassed shade of red lighting her fair skin. Jackson felt no such awkwardness about their exchange, only contentment settled in his chest. The love of his life was alive and in his arms, and he wanted everyone to know it.

"Can we finish this up now, please?" Gustafson asked, exasperation evident in his voice.

Jackson could have sworn he heard a little jealousy there, too.

Alicia wrapped her hands around his middle, holding on to Jackson with a tight grip as though she was worried he would disappear into thin air. He held on to her with equal desperation, longing for the time they could be alone together without the smirks and sidelong glances from the group. But this was important, too. This was closure.

The gathering of their collective of Hunters, Vampires, and Jody as the lone human observed the remains of a nightmare burned to ash. The flames heralded the beginning of an alliance between Hunters and Vampires.

CHAPTER TWENTY-EIGHT

Nora couldn't help the sappy smile pulling up the corners of her mouth any more than anyone else in the room could when they saw the exchange between Alicia and Jackson. She would even admit she may have shed a tear or two at their emotional reunion. Nora was pretty sure, had everyone not been there watching, the exchange would have turned a little more steamy.

Turning her gaze up to look at Endre, Nora remembered the suffering she'd endured when she thought she'd lost him and the overpowering relief when he'd found her again. Endre's eyes were already watching her, completely disinterested with the display in front of them. Nora had no desire to watch anymore either; the atmosphere of the room was filled with rage and anger, but also a slight undercurrent of mourning. She didn't think anyone here mourned Micelli, they mourned over the devastation and the lives changed by his alliance with Jaqueline.

But it was all a catch twenty-two. Without the interference of their villains, Nora and Endre would never have found one another when Micelli arranged from the shadows for her to dig him up from his grave. Jackson and Alicia wouldn't have met when Micelli's henchman tried to force her into his service. Even Zeke and Jody wouldn't have met had Micelli not invaded her home and Jackson sent Zeke to rescue her. Micelli and Jaqueline were the catalyst for three romantic relationships in this room, and now for an alliance—albeit somewhat new and shaky—between the Vampires and the Hunters.

It was difficult to feel any gratuity to their enemies for the destruction they wrought, but Nora could still appreciate the way the universe wove things together to balance out the bad with the good.

"What are you thinking?" Endre inquired curiously, his eyes searching hers.

"I'm trying to find the words to thank Micelli for introducing us," she whispered.

A soft chuckle interrupted the solemnity of the room. A few of the Hunters' heads turned to stare at them, their eyes cold and angry. It was plain to anyone they hated the Vampires they now parlayed with. Nora was sure they all had good reasons; they had each undoubtedly lost family members or comrades in the pursuit of exterminating Vampires. Nora also suspected when they looked at her, they saw the Vampire responsible for the lives of Hunters lost in the bunker Jackson helped her escape from. But she was no longer *really* a Vampire anymore. That wouldn't matter to them, though. 'Once a Vampire, always a Vampire' was surely their philosophy. And why wouldn't it be? Her situation was unprecedented.

"Let's get you up to the lab and begin some analysis," Endre encouraged, interpreting her change in mood as distress. He wasn't wrong, but what ailed her was emotional and not physical.

The throng in the room shifted as the flames died down, ready to move on to whatever lay ahead for them. One by one they shuffled up the stairs, the Vampires, human, and half-human moving toward the lab, and the Hunters to who knew where. They wouldn't be leaving the building though, Nora knew that. They would hang around until the cure reformulation was complete and then decisions would need to be made. Were the Vampires free to go? Would they help the Hunters distribute the cure? Would the Hunters merely execute the Vampires once they had what they wanted?

Endre helped Nora up onto the sterile metal table, the cold sending a shiver through her. Alicia approached through the door, Jackson's hand gripped in hers so tightly both their knuckles were white. The sight brought a small smile to Nora's face. Everyone deserved some happiness after the hell they'd all been through.

"I think maybe we should start with any observed changes you've noticed," Alicia said after taking a deep breath and extricating herself from Jackson.

"That is a very good place to start," Endre agreed, his tone decidedly less hostile toward the other woman than in the past.

Taking a deep breath, Nora tried to catalog in her mind what had changed and what hadn't, and where to start. Endre rubbed up and down her shoulders and handed her another of those horrible meal replacement shakes.

"I think you should drink another one of these before we start," Endre encouraged.

"Half," Jody corrected from across the room.

"I feel we have surpassed that, she could do a whole one," Endre argued, fixing the nurse with a hard glare.

"I think it would be better to start out slow. It's better to give her half doses at closer intervals than to try a full serving all at once and have something go wrong," Jody countered, raising her eyebrows at him in challenge.

"I am the doctor," Endre replied, his voice low and threatening.

"And a good doctor knows when to listen to the input of his experienced nursing staff," Jody challenged, her hands propped on hips, leveling a glare of her own at Endre.

Endre growled from beside Nora, and she had to suppress the urge to giggle at the exchange. He wasn't used to being challenged, but this group he was now surrounded with didn't seem to mind putting him in his place every now and then.

"Half," Endre reluctantly agreed.

"Let's not get everyone riled up," Alicia warned nervously, looking between the irate Vampire and her very human sister. Although, Nora was fairly certain if it came to violence, Jody would have three Vampires on her side against Endre. Endre glared at everyone in the room in turn, as if realizing his slim odds in a physical altercation.

"You might want something to write this down," Nora spoke up, breaking through the tension and handing Endre her half-full bottle of vanilla-flavored sludge.

"Right," Alicia agreed, scrambling around the room in search of a notebook and pen.

Waiting patiently, Nora noted the decline in tension in the room in everyone except Endre; he was practically vibrating with it from beside her. She placed her hand lightly on his arm.

"We're a team now," she reminded him, gesturing to the six of them in the room.

"I don't work well in a team," Endre admitted gruffly, his gaze locked on his clenched fists.

Nora reassuringly squeezed his arm. "I know, but we can't do this on our own."

"I suppose I will have to learn, then," Endre relented with a dour smile.

"Okay," Alicia interrupted breathlessly, holding up a notepad and a pen, "let's start with what you've noticed *hasn't* changed."

Nora leaned back into where Endre stood behind her on the table, using him for support. She began ticking off her list on her fingers. "I still have fangs. My hearing is just the same, so is my sight and sense of smell."

Alicia looked up from the notepad. "What about strength?"

"I don't know," Nora admitted with a shrug. It wasn't like she was nutritionally sound enough right now to find out.

"What about changes?" Alicia questioned, frowning down at where her pen scribbled on paper.

"Well, we saw the whole thing with my body eating itself."

"You look *much* better," Jody chimed in from across the room.

"Still a little thin," Endre added.

Nora turned to look at him with raised eyebrows. Well, she already knew he was a fan of her body before, but it appeared he definitely wasn't into the stick-thin models. That was good for her. She never aspired to be one.

"I agree, you look better." Alicia stuck the pen in her mouth while she sat deep in thought for a second. "How long had you gone between your last feeding and when you first had the meal supplement?"

"Um," Nora said, biting her lip and looking over at Jody thoughtfully. How long had they been in that room together?

"You fed the day before Micelli and company took over the lab," Jackson reminded her.

"Then that was it, so it was about two days since I'd had anything to eat or drink or whatever."

Alicia scribbled in her notepad. "Are you feeling a desire for blood?"

"No," Nora acknowledged.

"Does the smell of blood make you salivate or appeal to you at all?" she inquired, chewing on her lip, her expression hopeful.

"Nope."

"That's good," Alicia sighed, making more notes. "I can work with this. I'm going to need a blood sample though." The room went quiet and Alicia tensed up, then glanced at Jody. "Uh, Jody, can you draw the blood? I'm not sure I should." Uncertainty edged her voice.

"Absolutely," Jody replied with a smile.

Nora watched her wash her hands in the sink, then snap on a pair of gloves before rooting through the vials and needles for something suitable. With efficient movements, Jody gathered what was needed and sat before Nora. Nora directed her gaze at Endre while Jody pressed on the skin at the crook of her elbow and tied the tourniquet above the stick. Cold alcohol pads brushed over her skin and she prepared for the needle. Endre smiled down reassuringly at Nora, and she remembered how much she hated the sight of her own blood being drawn.

The initial poke of the needle wasn't as bad as Nora remembered it, but the coppery smell of her blood was more nauseating than she could recall. A hitch in Alicia's breath across the room brought Nora's attention to her. The Vampire's pupils had dilated significantly and her breathing grew erratic.

"I think I need to leave," Alicia informed them in a strained voice.

"Me too. I'll walk you out," Zeke offered, taking a long swallow, his eyes watching the little vial fill with Nora's blood.

Looking back at Endre, Nora held his gaze with worried eyes. How was Alicia going to work on the cure when she couldn't handle the sight or smell of blood?

CHAPTER TWENTY-NINE

Striding swiftly to the kitchenette, Alicia sucked in deep breaths, trying to quell the crazy reaction she had to watching Nora's blood being drawn. She knew she'd have cravings, but she had *no* idea it would be this bad. All along, she had been thinking it was going to be more like when she had a craving for chocolate when PMSy. She didn't think it would be full-blown drug addict craving. And the nausea, she didn't expect the nausea at all.

"It's intense, isn't it?" Zeke offered from beside her. Alicia barely registered he was lightly rubbing her back, the motion soothing.

"How do you handle it?" Alicia questioned, peering up at her sister's love interest.

"I can tell you it gets better over time, but it's always going to be hard. That's why we need your cure so much," he told her with a wan smile.

"Do you always feel like you're going to barf before you feed? That seems counter-productive."

Zeke's brow furrowed. "I never feel like I'm going to throw up."

"Weird," Alicia acknowledged, finally able to catch her breath.

"Ah, I see my timing is impeccable," a voice called from the doorway.

Gustafson lounged against the doorjamb casually. Alicia had been so wrapped up in her reaction, she hadn't even heard the leader of the Hunters approach. Her gaze zeroed in on the polystyrene cooler he held up and shook at her like she was a dog and he had a treat. She didn't particularly care for that parallel, but it was more than likely very close to his mindset.

"We didn't want you Vamps having to go out hunting when you could be here working on that cure." The Hunter tossed the cooler to Zeke, who caught it with little effort.

Alicia was pretty sure even as a Vampire she would have dropped that.

Zeke opened the cooler and handed Alicia a blood bag.

"Where did you get that?" Alicia gasped, looking down at the blood in her hand. Type A positive. She wondered if the different blood types would have different flavors. *How morbid.*

"I know a guy," was all Gustafson said before pushing off the casement with his shoulder and leaving her alone with Zeke again.

Alicia pulled at the plug sealing the bag and drank it like it was a fucking juice box. *People juice boxes.* She shuddered at the thought. She really needed to get working on that cure.

When she finished the bag, Alicia shoved the cooler into the fridge and turned to Zeke, arms crossed over her chest. She hadn't gotten a chance to really talk to him yet. Not wanting to sound too cliché, but she needed to know what his intentions were with Jody. Her *human* sister. Whose blood called to him like a drug, if Alicia's reaction to Nora's blood was any indication.

"So, you and my sister, huh?" Alicia tried to ask casually. She was pretty sure she failed—it came out more threatening than she intended.

Zeke cleared his throat and looked to the ceiling, as if searching for the best answer to placate her. That wasn't going to happen. She wanted truth, and she at least had the strength to beat it out of him if she wanted to. Well, he was probably still stronger than her. Maybe. Okay, *definitely* stronger than her. But Jackson would help her if she wanted him to, she was sure of that.

"I really care about Jody," Zeke carefully enunciated.

"Do you love her?" Alicia demanded.

It was a ridiculous question, Zeke couldn't love Jody. Not that Jody wasn't loveable and all, but they hardly knew each other!

But Jackson loves you.

Alicia reprimanded that inner voice. This was different. This was her little sister. What would their parents think if they knew she'd allowed her baby sister to cavort with a Vampire lover. Oh God, what would their parents think if they found out *she* was a Vampire.

"Are you okay?" Zeke worried, staring at her with wide eyes. "You just went white as a sheet."

"I'm a-a-a Vampire," Alicia stammered, collapsing into one of the chairs at the small table. "My parents are going to kill me!"

"I think it's too late for that, Al," Jody said from the doorway to the lab with a smile. "We're done in there if you want to come back in."

Alicia shook her head and peered up at Jody through unshed tears. "What if I can't fix this?" she whispered.

"Hey," Jody took the chair next to her, "don't let doubt take over now. Look at what you've already done."

"I've created something that's eating Nora from the inside," Alicia bawled, dropping her head into her hands and allowing her sobs to escape.

"Sweetie," Jody soothed softly, rubbing between Alicia's shoulder blades. It *should* have been soothing, but with her heightened senses and heightened emotions, it felt like a million tiny needles assaulting her nerves. "We haven't even looked yet to see what exactly the changes were. The emaciation may not be an ongoing thing. We'll figure it out, it will be okay. *You'll* be okay."

Pulling in a deep breath, Alicia came to a decision she'd been struggling with since she woke up. She loved her sister. She wanted to protect her. Staying in a converted hospital with an overabundance of supernatural beings was not the best way to protect Jody.

"There is no 'we' here, Jo. You need to leave. Go stay with Mom and Dad until I get this sorted out," Alicia ordered sternly. She even threw in her best no-nonsense expression, complete with pursed lips.

Jody jerked back, the action and her expression looking as though Alicia had slapped her.

"No. I'm staying," Jody argued.

"This is not up for discussion," Alicia ground out through gritted teeth. Why couldn't she see she was trying to keep her safe and out of this world? She'd failed once when Micelli got his hands on her, she wasn't about to make the same mistake twice.

"I am just as much a part of this now as you are!" Jody yelled, tears brimming along her lower lids. "I want to help. I *am* helping. I have just as much of a vested interest in this as you do."

"This is about keeping you safe!" Alicia argued.

"Those that were a threat are gone. Dead. Ash. Who exactly are you trying to keep me safe from? Zeke? He saved me. He had every opportunity to hurt me, kill me even, if he wanted to. Your friends? If they wanted me dead, I'd *be* dead," Jody hollered, pointing to each of the Vampires in turn.

"Me! I'm worried *I* will hurt you," Alicia blurted out, vocalizing the concern she couldn't identify until now. "I don't know if I can control myself. This is new. It hurts. It's hard. I don't know if I have the control."

"We're right here to help you," Jackson's soft voice spoke into her ear, his hands warm on her shoulders.

"*All* of us," Jody said stubbornly. "I'm staying."

Silence filled the small kitchenette packed with too many bodies. Alicia glanced from one face to the next. It seemed no one was willing to take her side on this. Leave it to Jody to steal the hearts of a pack of Vampires.

"Fine. It seems I can't make you go. But I want you to promise me something," Alicia began, pausing, waiting for Jody's response.

Jody sat watching her silently. When Alicia didn't continue, Jody scoffed. "I know you. I'm not promising anything until I know what it is."

The smirk lifting the corner of Alicia's mouth came unbidden. She should have known Jody wouldn't give the typical response of 'anything,' knowing how Alicia would twist it to get what she wanted.

"Promise me you'll keep your bodyguard close," Alicia conceded, looking up to where Zeke stood behind Jody, hands planted protectively on her shoulders.

"That won't be a problem," Zeke answered for Jody, his gaze turning to the object of his affection.

Although he never answered Alicia's question earlier if he was in love with her sister, he didn't have to. The expression on his face said it all. Complete devotion and adoration. Alicia had seen it enough on Endre's face when he looked at Nora. She glanced to where Jackson stood behind her, mirroring the position of Jody and Zeke. That look was in his expression, too, as he gazed down at her.

"Are the siblings done squabbling yet?" Endre sighed from the doorway to the lab.

Well, at least one thing seemed the same. Endre was as ornery as the moment Alicia met him.

CHAPTER THIRTY

"You've been in here for hours, it's time to take a break," Jackson said, looking down at where Alicia sat hunched over a microscope, jotting down notes every few minutes.

The moment the blood sample had been ready, she launched into work with fervor. The guilt rolling off her was palpable. Alicia placed the entirety of the blame for Nora's reaction to the serum on her own shoulders, though each of the four of them had a hand in its formulation.

"Just give me a few more minutes," she droned, not bothering to look up from her microscope.

That shit wasn't going to fly with Jackson. He wasn't going to let her burn herself out over this. He'd worked on it for months with Endre and Nora, he knew how absorbing the work could be and how quickly one could get lost in it if they weren't careful.

"Nope, you're taking a break," he commanded, turning her stool so she faced him.

Her eyes were tired and bloodshot. Her shoulders drooped. This wasn't how he wanted to see her—worried, over-worked, and exhausted.

"Jackson," she protested weakly, rolling her shoulders and cracking her neck.

Jackson removed her hands from where they rubbed at the base of her skull. That was his job. His fingers ghosted over the delicate skin then increased the pressure where he felt knots. Alicia's head lolled forward while he worked his magic down her neck and over her shoulders. He knew anatomy well and used it to his advantage when pressing his fingers into her tired muscles. A low moan escaped her when he pressed into the flesh along her vertebrae at her lower back; the sound shot his blood flowing straight to his cock. It was time to take this break in a different direction.

"I know a way to relax you," he whispered huskily in her ear, relishing the way his breath across her skin sent a shiver through her body.

"Yeah?" she questioned casually, although her body's response was anything but.

There was some benefit to being a Vampire, namely, at this moment, knowing *exactly* how aroused Alicia was. Her heart rate increased, as did her breathing. Then there was the alluring scent of her arousal. Even through layers of clothing the perfume of her desire permeated his nostrils, pushing any kind of thoughts he had that were not of her to the side.

"Yeah," he answered, scooping her up and carrying her through the door.

"Jackson, I can't just leave my sample," Alicia protested … her high brain function apparently more intact than his was.

"Yes, you can," Jackson countered, not once breaking his urgent stride toward their room. *Theirs*. Together. He liked that.

Jackson had barely closed the door behind them before he'd removed his clothing and half of hers. His lips roamed over her exposed chest, reveling in the creamy soft skin and the chill bumps his breath left in its wake. Pulling the erect peak of one breast into his mouth, his fingers tugged and twisted the other. Sucking at the nipple, he toyed with it with his tongue and grinned at the little sounds of pleasure escaping from her. He *loved* those sounds. He lived for them. They reminded him he could have gone the rest of his life not hearing them ever again when he thought she was gone. Now that she was alive, he wanted to hear them every day.

Alicia's hands roamed over his shoulders and down his pecs while he continued to lavish her breasts with attention. Her short nails scraped over stiffened nipples and he nipped at hers in response. Low, animalistic sounds came from her, and Jackson didn't know how much longer he could continue foreplay before he gave in to his desperation to be inside of her.

"Jackson, I *need* you," she groaned.

Her hands explored down over his taut abs, nails outlining every peak and valley he worked hard to maintain. From there, the roving hands stopped, and a frustrated growl escaped her when she couldn't reach her destination.

"Yeah?" he asked playfully around her nipple.

"Yes!" she cried out adamantly when he nibbled at the swell of her breast.

He trailed soft kisses down over her belly toward the alluring scent of womanhood, needing at least a taste before he gave her what she wanted. Her fingers tugged at his hair desperately, little quivers running through her body with each press of his lips. When he reached just above the waistband of her scrubs, he ran a teasing finger underneath it, barely brushing the light patch of hair beneath. With a grin, he watched the anguished expression on her face—her mouth hung open slightly, her eyes squeezed shut, cheeks a rosy pink with arousal. When he didn't rip her pants off like she clearly expected, her eyes popped open and she fixed him with a steely glare.

"If you don't take my pants off, I'm going to have to hurt you," she growled at him, the sound somehow making him harder.

A wide grin split Jackson's face while he inched her pants down over her hips, his eyes never leaving her glaring ones.

"I swear to God, or whatever omnipotent being there might be, that I will break something if you keep teasing me," she threatened.

"Aren't you demanding," Jackson chuckled.

All of their other encounters had been frantic, desperate acts with a short timetable. They had time now and he was damned well going to use it to wring every ounce of pleasure from her he could. He had to show her there was plenty good about being a Vampire … starting with the amazing sex.

Alicia lifted her hips, encouraging him to slide the fabric over the swell of her amazing ass. He'd make a mental note to take her from behind at least once tonight so he could get some nice handfuls of those cheeks. The moment the scrubs peeled away from her hot center, Jackson could feel his control slipping. He ripped the pants the rest of the way down her legs in frantic tugs, revealing his goddess in all her naked glory. Holy. Fucking. Shit. And she was *his*.

Jackson dipped his head, taking in a lungful of the scent of her arousal. That was there, for *him*. Dragging his tongue through her drenched slit, he gathered the moisture there and dissected the taste like a fine wine. Sweet. Salty. Musky. All mixed together? Perfection.

"Mmmm," he hummed his appreciation at her taste. He needed more.

Swirling his tongue around her clit and back down to spear her entrance, Jackson gathered up more of the sweet nectar. He continued to work this tongue through her folds, alternating pressure and patterns. Each sweep brought an abundance of mewling and panting noises from Alicia which had grown steadily louder with the duration of his ministrations. Her muscles grew tighter, and he knew she was close. A much as he wanted to feel the contractions milking his cock, he wanted to taste her release more. He was fairly confident he could bring her to the edge again with little effort and experience her climax from inside later. Maybe even a few times.

"Jackson. Jackson, I'm going to come," she cried out urgently.

Not bothering to answer with words, he let his mouth show her what he wanted.

Alicia's entire body seized and she let out a keening cry even the non-Vampires in the building were sure to hear. Jackson couldn't contain his smile of pride; he'd done that, he'd pushed her over the edge and pulled that sound from her. Continuing to lick gently, he elicited tiny twitches from her with every pass over her sensitive nub. She collapsed limply onto the bed and smiled down at him with glassy eyes and rosy cheeks.

"You're so fucking beautiful," he whispered, watching the red in her cheeks deepen.

Covering her face with her hands, Alicia gave a nervous giggle. It was cute and endearing. God, he loved this woman. He was going to make sure she knew it and remembered it, too.

Jackson crawled up her body, a predatory glint in his eye. Alicia had seen in there before, but this time she was of the same breed—not just the prey. He dipped his head to press his lips to hers and she lifted to meet him halfway. His lips and teeth devoured her mouth, and she tasted the musk of her release on him. Not that she particularly enjoyed the taste, but it was a reminder of the pleasure Jackson had pulled from her with just his mouth.

"Where do you want me?" she offered, playing the part of the prey ... for the moment. She wondered how he'd fuck her now that she wasn't a fragile human anymore. The thought of having him completely unbridled sent a quiver of anticipation through her.

"Right here," he whispered, trailing kisses down her neck, his fangs pressing lightly into her flesh but not drawing blood. A little shiver ran through her, surprising her with the excitement she felt at the thought of him biting her.

Feeling bold, Alicia nipped back at his shoulder using her own fangs, but she *did* draw blood. She licked the droplets off her lip while he watched, completely enraptured.

"We'll get to that later, there's something else more *pressing*," Jackson emphasized, his voice husky. Looking down between their bodies, he drew Alicia's gaze to where his hard cock sat heavily between their bodies.

Instinctively, Alicia spread her legs wider, giving him greater access. Jackson growled at the sight of her spread before him, and in one quick thrust buried himself to the hilt. Throwing her head back, she absorbed the ecstasy of being so full. Jackson's thrusts were gentle and measured, sweet. Maybe she'd want sweet another time, but right now, she wanted to see what sex between two otherworldly creatures felt like.

"Harder," she whispered, feeling her face go red with the wanton request. She'd never been a dirty talker—it was definitely foreign territory for her—but she figured seeing as she was now a totally new being, why not branch out and grow … embrace the wantonness.

Jackson groaned and did as she requested, his hips slamming into hers at a bruising pace she was loving every moment of. She hoped she bruised, though she'd likely never see them before they healed. He hooked his hands beneath her knees and angled her hips up, the new position earning him a gasp. Each drag in and out hit just right inside, and she could feel an orgasm building, even without clitoral stimulation. That was a rarity for her.

Each thrust sent Alicia climbing higher and higher toward another climax. Just when she was right on the edge, Jackson gave her a wicked grin. *Uh oh.* She was in trouble. He licked his thumb and with one stroke over her bundle of nerves, sent her flying over that precipice.

"Jackson!" Alicia screamed out, both in pleasure and anguish.

"That's right, let everyone know who's making you come," he taunted. All sense of embarrassment left her. With all the Vampires in the building, there was *no* way they weren't hearing this all from the start. "I need to see that ass now."

Alicia didn't really have the powers of observation at the moment to realize Jackson had pulled out until she was flipped onto her stomach. She didn't really have any control of her muscles either, so when Jackson pulled her up so her ass was in the air, she could barely hold the position, her legs were shaking so badly. She didn't have to, though; Jackson kept his hold on her, not allowing her to fall—first with his arm around her waist while he placed kisses up her back, then with his hands gripping her hips when he filled her again.

"Give me another one, I want to feel you come on my cock," Jackson demanded, placing her hand between her legs.

Well, she wasn't going to say no to that. Alicia rubbed with a vigorous tempo, matching the pace of Jackson's ardent thrusts. His calloused hands squeezed and kneaded her cheeks. Breaths growing heavier, his thrusts grew more erratic, and Alicia could tell he was close. She increased her pace and let another orgasm rush through her, but apparently Jackson wasn't finished. Once again he flipped her to her back and she was glad—she wanted to see him lose all inhibitions in the throes of pleasure.

"I want to see you when I come," he told her, giving a few more thrusts before he let out a roar. When he collapsed atop her, still pulsing inside, he sank his fangs into her shoulder.

A surprised gasp escaped Alicia when he slowly eased those sharp implements into her skin. There had been the initial pain when they punctured, but it soon dissipated to slight pressure. Jackson gripped the back of her neck and guided her mouth to his shoulder, mirroring the location of where he drank from her. Hesitantly, Alicia sank her fangs into his flesh, his blood filling her mouth. This was her first foray into drinking blood from something other than a beaker or blood bag. And she had to admit, the predator now a part of her loved the rush of warm blood flooding her mouth and trickling down her throat.

They lay like that, feeding from one another for some time. Alicia had no idea how long, the euphoria erasing the concept of time from her brain entirely. When Jackson finally pulled his fangs from her, she'd gotten so used to the pressure of his pull she whimpered at the loss. He chuckled and smoothed her hair from her face. She didn't want to let go, but figured it might be bad form if she didn't. She didn't exactly know the etiquette for simultaneous Vampire drinking. All she knew was that next to the phenomenal sex, it was the most pleasurable feeling she'd ever experienced.

Alicia slowly slid her fangs from his shoulder, licking at any errant droplets of blood that had the audacity to escape her mouth. Her fingers ghosted over the puncture wounds, admiring her handiwork. She liked seeing her mark on him. It was a pity they would heal. Just as she had, Jackson was running rough fingers over the marks he'd made, a strange expression on his face.

"Marry me," he whispered, turning his gaze from her shoulder to her face.

"Come again?" Alicia knew technically she was a Vampire and could hear things very well, but she wasn't entirely certain she *understood* what he had just said.

"Well, I think I need to recover a little first, but I could go for another round," he offered with a smirk. *Smartass*. "I want to be with you. For as long as we have together. Human, Hunter, Vampire, I don't care. Just be with me?"

All Alicia could do was stare at him with wide eyes. *Is this real? Any of it?*

"I can't tell what you're thinking," he worried, a deep furrow between his brows.

"Yes. Absolutely, yes," Alicia laughed.

Holy shit, I'm engaged!

"I don't have a ring yet, but I'll get you one," Jackson promised. "Whatever you want … a huge diamond, platinum, whatever you want."

"I don't even need a ring, as long as I have you," she breathed out, a gigantic smile plastered on her face. "I know that's really corny or cliché, or whatever, but it's true."

"Oh, you'll get a ring. I don't want there to be any doubt you're mine," he proclaimed, a possessive glint in his eyes.

"Well, then since these won't stay long," Alicia said, running fingers over the bite marks on his shoulder, "I want everyone to know you belong to me, too."

"I fucking love you," Jackson whispered, crushing her with a hug.

"I fucking love you, too," Alicia giggled. Jackson pressed kisses to every inch of her face while she continued to giggle.

"Get some rest, because when you wake up, you're going to fuck your fiancé," he promised with a devious grin. She liked the sound of that. Both the fiancé part and the fucking part.

CHAPTER THIRTY-ONE

"Wake up, wife," Jackson whispered into Alicia's ear.

Alicia smiled at his words, even though she wanted nothing to do with waking. Her sleep had been fitful and filled with grotesque images from blood memories of Jackson getting the shit beat out of him. Alicia was pretty damned sure she was going to break every appendage on every single one of the Hunters roaming around the building.

"I need more sleep," she moaned, trying to pull the covers over her head.

"Up." He whisked the blankets off her body entirely.

"Nooooo," Alicia whined, tucking herself into the fetal position.

"I'm going to enjoy waking up to this every morning," Jackson confessed huskily, his hands roaming over her naked body, now officially waking up every part of her.

"Me too." She smiled, stretching so she was open for him. His touch set her on fire and she was ready to wake up if it meant having him inside of her again. *Her fiancé.* It had a nice ring to it.

Jackson let out a groan, his eyes drawn to the apex of her thighs spread wide. Gentle fingers brushed along her over-heated flesh.

"Fuck, Alicia," he growled.

"Yes," she whispered in response, her voice thick with growing lust. What was he waiting for?

"I want you so bad, but I'm going to have to take a raincheck." His voice was filled with regret.

"What?" Alicia asked, her confusion apparent.

"We need to get to the lab, everyone's waiting for us. We overslept," Jackson explained apologetically.

"Dammit." Rolling to the edge of the bed, she climbed to her feet. A wave of nausea rolled through her and she had to throw her hands out to steady herself against the wall.

Jackson was at her side immediately. "You all right?"

Holding her hand on her stomach, Alicia tried not to puke on the floor. "I don't feel so great."

"Maybe the blood swap was too intense," Jackson offered, sitting her back on the bed. "Give it a minute."

Alicia nodded, but that was a bad idea, the movement just made the nausea worse. She sat on the edge of the bed while Jackson eased her into scrubs. It felt simultaneously weird and nice to have someone take care of her.

"We'll get you a blood bag when we go through the kitchen," he advised, pulling her to her feet by her hand. "You okay to walk?"

"I think so." She took deep breaths to quell the need to vomit. She could already feel her mouth watering, heralding the upcoming contents of her stomach. "Can I drink water? Do Vampires drink water?" she asked urgently.

"Here." Jackson pressed a glass of cool water into her hand and she began to chug it. "Slow down or it's all going to come back up."

Slowing her gulps to sips, Alicia finished half the glass of water before handing it back to Jackson. The churning in her guts subsiding for the time being.

"Thanks," she told him gratefully. "Is that normal?"

"I've never experienced that before, but your whole transition has been unusual," Jackson admitted, letting out a heavy breath. "We better go before Endre comes to drag us out of here."

The walk to the lab was slow, Alicia afraid any sudden movements might prompt the expulsion of the contents of her stomach, although, she was pretty damned sure there wasn't much other than water in there. As promised, Jackson grabbed a blood bag from the fridge and handed it to her, but even the sight of it made her want to hurl.

"I'll have it later," she refused, handing it back to him quickly before the mere sight of it sent her running for the nearest toilet. Or the sink. The sink would do in an emergency. Beggars can't be choosers, after all.

"About time," Endre grumbled when they finally made their way through the door. "Long night?" he queried, his voice definitely containing a taunt.

"A *very* long night," Alicia acknowledged weakly, but managed to give Endre a saucy wink.

Alicia figured that ought to shut him up when he figured out he wasn't going to be embarrassing her. A hearty laugh rumbled through him, and she saw him smile. Again.

"I didn't know his mouth could do that," Alicia gasped with amazement to Nora.

"I know, right?" Nora chuckled, shaking her head, but smiling at Endre just the same.

"All right, now that we've established my sister is a hussy," Jody remarked with a smirk, "I propose we draw another sample of blood to compare with the last one."

"What exactly are we comparing, doctor?" Endre questioned, his tone teasing.

Endre teasing. Alicia figured he must have gotten some last night, too, because he seemed to be in an exceptionally good mood.

"Nora's been properly fed and hydrated for another twenty-four hours since the last blood draw, so I think it would be prudent to compare her nutrient levels and blood cell counts," Jody answered, unfazed by Endre's teasing barb.

"Properly fed is up for debate," grumbled Nora as she glared sourly at the meal replacement shake in her hand.

Everyone in the room joined in a little chuckle, except Alicia. It seemed everyone was in a fantastic mood today except her. Usually she was the upbeat and positive one in the mornings, cracking jokes and trying to lighten the atmosphere in a heavy situation, especially if it was before everyone had coffee. She was going to miss coffee.

"You okay?" Jody worried, looking her up and down.

"I'm not feeling great," Alicia answered, her stomach continuing to roil.

"A little too much f—" Endre didn't get to finish his undoubtedly crude comment before Nora elbowed him in the gut.

"Let's get this blood sample over with," Nora redirected the conversation.

"You want to do it, or you want me to?" Jody asked Alicia, eying her warily.

"You can do it," Alicia offered without hesitation. Just the thought of the smell of blood made her nearly flee the room.

Jody gathered the equipment and started the process. The minute the needle pierced Nora's skin, Alicia was running for the door, hoping she could make it to the sink in the kitchenette.

CHAPTER THIRTY-TWO

Jackson watched Alicia pull away from the microscope and rub her eyes. He checked the time, then continued to watch her. He was giving her another five minutes, and then dragging her back to bed to sleep. This nausea bullshit was starting to worry him. For the last three days, she'd hardly fed at all, and most of what she did take in came back up fairly quickly. He was *this* close to hooking her up to a damn IV just to make sure she didn't wither away.

"You know, it's really unnerving having you stare at me like that while I'm trying to work," she murmured, her face pressed back to that fucking microscope.

"How are you feeling? Any appetite today?" he inquired, watching her expression carefully for any signs she might respond to the affirmative to placate him.

Letting out a deep sigh, Alicia turned to him. "Not really."

"How about the nausea?"

"Still there." Her annoyance rang through loud and clear. "And it will continue to be there, even with you hovering over me like this." Yep, she was definitely annoyed with him.

"I'm worried about you," Jackson confessed, getting up from his stool and standing behind her. He massaged the tense muscles in her shoulders, earning him a little groan. "You're working too hard."

"No, I'm not working hard enough," Alicia protested.

"We're in no rush here. Nora is doing well, she's improving every day. I bet she's almost strong enough to kick Endre's ass again," Jackson chuckled.

"Not in a rush? You mean you enjoy the armed Hunters parading through the building like we're on some military lockdown? Because I certainly don't!" she snapped, jerking forward to pull her body from beneath his hands. Jackson eyed her warily like a ticking time bomb poised to explode at any moment. He'd never seen her act this way. "And what about what's happening to me?" There it was, the thing eating away at her … literally.

"We'll figure it out," he soothed, reaching for her shoulders again, wanting to do at least something to ease her tension.

"Don't patronize me!" Alicia yelled, rising from her stool so he could no longer reach her.

"I think it's time for you to take a break," Jackson told her in low tones. She was clearly overworked and stressed out, and he couldn't see how that would be any help to her current condition.

"Don't touch me," she hissed when he reached for her.

Jackson slowly took a step back from the woman clearly on the edge. He wanted to subdue her, but felt maybe a gentler hand was needed. He was losing his patience and was worried he might just stick her with a needle to sedate her, and he at least had the foresight to know that wouldn't go over well. He needed another strategy.

"Where are you going?" she asked, her voice panicked.

He didn't understand at all. She didn't want him to touch her. She wouldn't let anyone help her. But she was in a frenzy because he was leaving after she practically bit his head off?

"I'm getting your sister. Maybe Jody can figure out what's going on with you … or at least talk some sense into you," he called over his shoulder before bursting from the lab.

Alicia slumped back onto her stool, watching Jackson's retreating back.

"What the hell is wrong with me?" she cried to the empty lab.

She didn't understand anything about what was happening to her. The transition should be straightforward, and from the sounds of it, none of the other Vampires had experienced similar symptoms to what she was enduring when they went through the change. It didn't make sense. But there wasn't time to worry about her problem, she had to fix this formulation of the cure so she could give it to the others. Based on what was happening with her, she had no idea if it was even going to work on her. She pulled up digital images of the samples. By now, she'd gathered samples of everyone's blood for comparison, even Jody's as a control.

"Hey Al," Jody called cheerfully as she walked into the lab. Alicia had lived with her long enough to see through the ruse. She already knew Jackson sent her, what was the point in pretending? "How is the formulation coming?"

Glancing down at her notebook, Alicia bit her lip. She debated how much to divulge to her sister. Everything Alicia had discovered was scribbled in the notebook and she had been guarding it with her life. Maybe it *was* time to let someone else help her.

"I've figured out a way to lessen the effects of the reversal so they aren't quite so dramatic. Now that we know the administration of the serum puts the body in starvation mode, we can be prepared for that with immediate nutritional support. The blood thirst should be virtually non-existent, but it seems the other physical Vampire traits are here to stay."

"That's great!" Jody exclaimed, bouncing on the stool next to Alicia's with a little clap. "Why don't you look excited about this?" Jody asked when she noticed Alicia wasn't celebrating.

"Because it won't work on Jackson," she whispered, her eyes brimming with tears.

"What do you mean it won't work on him?"

"There's an anomaly from his Hunter genes. I need to come up with something entirely different for him, but I just can't figure it out," Alicia managed to get out before breaking into hysterical sobs.

"Oh, honey, we'll work together, all of us. We'll figure this out," Jody crooned, pulling Alicia into a hug. She sure was damn tired of hearing they would all figure this out. They didn't figure it out without her before, how would they do it now when she was struggling so much?

"Is that what's got you so worked up?" Jackson's voice echoed through the lab. Alicia had almost forgotten he didn't have to be in the room to hear the conversation. "Jody's right, *we* will figure it out. You don't have to do this on your own. There's no need to hold up the production of the serum for everyone else because of me."

"I won't take it until there's something for you, too," Alicia sniffled adamantly.

"You're damn right you will," Jackson protested. "You need it more than anyone. Your body is rejecting the change, it's not allowing you to feed. It's imperative you take that serum."

"He's right," Jody chimed in.

"But what if we never figure something out for you? Would you still want to be married to me and watch me die?" Alicia choked on the last word. They were supposed to take the next steps in their lives together.

"You're getting married? How come you didn't tell me?" Jody gasped from beside her.

Alicia turned to glare at her sister. Her heart was breaking over leaving Jackson alone in the world, and her sister was concerned she hadn't shared the secret yet?

"I've been a little preoccupied," Alicia snapped. Jody's face contorted into an expression of pain. "I'm sorry," Alicia apologized, her voice softening. "I'm just … I don't even know. Sick, tired, stressed out, take your pick."

"I know," Jody whispered back, avoiding looking at her. Not that Alicia could blame her. She was being a complete bitch to the people who were here to help her.

"I think I do need to rest." Clearly she was in no state to continue working tonight.

"We'll continue working tomorrow night. I'm going to make sure you get a full day's sleep," Jackson warned, helping Alicia to her feet. She was grateful for his support, both literally and figuratively. She wasn't sure her exhausted body could hold her weight if she tried.

Nodding wearily, Alicia allowed Jackson to lead her toward their room. She didn't know how he could stand to even be near her with how she'd acted. When he had her tucked into bed, her eyes heavy with the effort to keep them open, he sat on the bed and petted her hair, clearly not intending to join her in it. Alicia opened her mouth to apologize or beg him to hold her, she wasn't sure which, but Jackson spoke first.

"I have an idea I think might help with getting you blood," he offered, the soothing touch of his hands through her hair lulling her closer to sleep.

"Hmmm?" She didn't even have the energy to form words anymore.

"How would you feel if we tried to administer the blood intravenously?"

Alicia's heavy eyelids opened as wide as her exhaustion would allow. The suggestion was intriguing and she was all out of other ideas. It was worth a shot. Anything to quell the nausea, ravenous hunger, and violent mood swings.

"You want to try it?" Jackson prompted, clearly looking for a response with more substance than raised eyebrows.

The nodding of her too-heavy head was about as good as he was going to get right now.

"Get some sleep, I'll have everything ready when you wake," Jackson whispered into her hair when he pressed a kiss to the top of her head.

He didn't even have to issue the order, she was already out.

CHAPTER THIRTY-THREE

It worked. It actually worked. Alicia watched Jackson pull the IV needle from her arm; he didn't even need to press a cotton ball to the little red dot before it disappeared within seconds. Sure, it took longer to take a blood bag this way, but it was better than nothing. Considering how *good* she felt, she would contend with an administration of blood intravenously every few days if it meant she wasn't barfing every time a drop of *anything* hit her stomach.

Today marked the third round of sucking blood through her arm instead of her teeth. Alicia pretended she was once again a poor college student donating plasma. It felt about the same as she remembered, at least the same pressure from when they put the blood, minus the plasma, back in. This particular procedure she not only got to keep her plasma, but welcomed someone else's life into her veins.

"How do you feel?" Jackson queried, watching her carefully.

"Fantastic," she declared with a smile. And she meant it.

"How have the blood memories been?" he questioned, examining her with a clinical eye.

Alicia didn't like it when he did that. His face took on a cold, calculating look. She preferred the warm, loving Jackson she saw every night when they awoke together in bed.

"Good," she hedged. The hard set of Jackson's mouth called bullshit without even uttering the words.

What else was she supposed to say? There were all kinds of memories from not only the good people who donated their blood to whatever facility the Hunters were swiping it from, but also Jackson's constant stream of getting the shit kicked out of him? Every night when she woke after one of those gory scenes, it took every ounce of self-control—and that was a lot—not to march through the halls and rip the Hunters apart piece by piece.

"They didn't have all the information," Jackson told her, as if reading her mind. Or she said something aloud.

"Stop doing that mind-reading thing, it freaks me out," she scolded.

"It doesn't take much to see what's going through your mind when you wear it so plainly on your face," he chuckled with raised eyebrows.

"Fine. I won't kill anyone. But just know I will never stand idly by in real life while they do that to *anyone*. Vampire, human, Hunter, it doesn't matter."

"I would never expect you to." Smirking, Jackson placed a kiss on her forehead. Okay, he won with that kiss.

"Are you ready for today?" Alicia asked excitedly, bouncing in her chair.

"Still having mood swings, I see," Endre lamented, walking through the door with Nora in tow.

"Still an asshole, I see," Alicia replied back, batting her eyelashes at him sweetly. "I'm just choosing to think on positive things instead of how I want to kick some people's asses."

"That, I would like to see," Zeke chuckled, wrapping his arms around Jody.

Alicia had been watching the two of them for the nearly two weeks they'd all been sequestered in the building by the Hunters. It was evident Zeke cared a great deal about her sister, so she couldn't hate him too much, even after the scandalous blood memories she had of them *together*. That was traumatizing to say the least.

"Tonight's the night, huh?" Jody smiled, seeming more content than Alicia was pretty sure she'd ever seen her. Like, *ever*.

"Yep, I finally get to stab Endre!" Alicia laughed, winking over in the general direction of Nora covering her mouth to stifle a giggle.

"As long as I get to administer the serum to you," Endre countered, continuing their banter. Awww, he was the like the brother she never wanted.

"Hold up, everyone. I am going to be the only one stabbing anyone with needles," Jody warned, giving everyone who might attempt to dispute a hard glare.

"She just wants to be involved since she won't be getting injected with anything," Zeke explained, a laugh escaping him when Jody smacked his arm.

Alicia liked this, the playful atmosphere that had developed over the last few days. Everyone was excited about what their future without thirst for blood held, and she couldn't blame them. However, no one had broached the difficult topics of what exactly that looked like.

Jody rubbed her hands together and gave her best villain face, complete with creepy grin and eyes watching everyone from beneath lowered brows. "Who wants to go first? Alicia? Would you like the honors?"

Alicia glanced up to Jackson who stood at her side. His face was a mask containing a reassuring smile, but it was clear there was concern beneath the façade.

"Should we get some of the Hunters in here," she wondered aloud, swallowing hard, saying anything to stall the inevitable.

"Present and accounted for," Gustafson announced from the doorway.

How none of the Vampires heard him was beyond Alicia. She supposed they were all so pumped up their attention was focused elsewhere.

"Al, it will be just fine," Jody coaxed, gathering a syringe and a vial in her gloved hands.

Alicia took a deep breath to relax. It was only fair she was the first to go in case something went horribly wrong. It was her formulation, after all.

"All right," she determined blowing out another breath.

"Excellent," Jody declared in her best impression of Mr. Burns from *The Simpsons*.

"That's not reassuring, Jo," Alicia muttered while Jody swabbed her arm with an alcohol laden cotton ball.

"Here goes nothing," Jody whispered.

"Wait!" Nora's frantic voice stopped Jody short of sticking the needle in Alicia's arm. "Do you hear that?"

CHAPTER THIRTY-FOUR

The room grew silent; no one quite sure what they were supposed to be listening for.

"What are we listening for?" Jody questioned, concern and confusion written across her face. Alicia imagined it was exactly how her face looked right about now.

"A heartbeat," Jackson whispered in awe, staring at Alicia wide-eyed.

In fact, everyone was staring at her. Alicia quickly glanced to each face in the room to confirm. Yep, everyone was looking at her. Except Nora. Nora was looking at her stomach. Oh no. Nope. No. It wasn't possible. There was no way that extra heartbeat was coming from her. There absolutely was *not* a baby in there.

"I am so confused right now. Can someone please tell me what's going on? You're all freaking me out," Jody worried, her voice wavering.

Zeke leaned in close to whisper in her ear, but they all could still hear, "I think you're going to be an auntie."

"What!" Jody's attention swung Alicia's way, big, blue eyes mirroring her own.

"I thought …" Alicia took a second to catch her breath. "I thought you said Vampires can't have, you know, one of these?" She pointed to her midsection.

"Jackson's not one hundred percent Vampire," Endre offered. "You said so yourself when you determined he needed a different formulation of the serum, he still retained some of his Hunter genes."

"You got me pregnant with a Vampire-Hunter baby?" Alicia accused Jackson, not sure her eyes would ever *not* be bugging out of her head.

Jackson's mouth gaped open but no sound issued forth. He was just as bewildered as she was. Of course he was. What were they going to do? What would this baby be like?

"That's why you didn't die!" Jody burst out. "I don't understand all the mechanics of it, but you must have been already pregnant when you were shot. It makes sense. Well, I mean, none of this *really* makes sense, but it kind of does. Oh my God, Al, you're going to have a baby! Jackson's baby! Did you know?" She leveled the last question at Jackson. "Is that why you proposed?"

"You proposed?" Nora echoed, a huge smile drawing up the corners of her mouth.

"No, I didn't know," Jackson acknowledged numbly, shaking his head.

"Are you freaking out just as much as I am?" Alicia asked him. Again, no words, but she got a nod. "Has this ever happened before?" Alicia directed her question to Endre.

"I have never heard anything like this before," Endre admitted, the expression on his face just as surprised as everyone else's.

"So, what is it going to be? A Vampire? A Hunter? Some kind of hybrid thing?" Alicia panicked, waving her hands around frantically. She didn't know the first thing about babies, let alone a Vampire-Hunter baby.

"Don't call your baby an 'it'," Jody scolded.

"Considering it's less than three weeks old and I only just found out about it a few minutes ago, it's still an *it*!" Alicia protested.

"Calm down, your hysterics can't be good for the baby." Jody shook her head. She was definitely in Nurse Jody mode now.

"I think I'm allowed to be a little hysterical!" Alicia waved her hands frantically in the air. "For fuck's sake, I'm pregnant! I'm a pregnant Vampire!"

"You can't take the serum," Endre pointed out, rather unhelpfully as far as Alicia was concerned. "If the serum wouldn't work for Jackson, it would hurt the baby, too."

"Jackson, are you okay?" Nora asked.

Alicia looked over to where Nora rubbed a hand along the back of a very pale-looking Jackson.

"I'm going to be a dad," he whispered to the floor, then met Alicia's eyes. "Holy fucking shit."

"Ditto," Alicia agreed, blowing out a breath.

"Well, this is entertaining," Gustafson laughed from the doorway.

Alicia leveled narrowed eyes at him, wishing she had something to throw.

The chances of hitting him were slim—even with Vampire prowess—but she was willing to take on the odds right now, considering her multi-anomaly status.

"Fuck you, asshole," Jackson shot at Gustafson, but there was no heat in it and a broad smile stretched across his face.

Jackson almost appeared to be happy. *Was* he happy about this? Was *she*? Alicia decided she need a little more time to let it all sink in before she could decide one way or another.

"Can we get on with what we came here for?" Endre asked, his voice bored.

"You are so insensitive," Jody scolded.

Endre shrugged. At least he knew he was a prick.

Jody held out her hand for Endre's arm—he extended it out to her. Without preamble or even proper cleaning Jody stabbed him viciously with the needle and pressed the plunger down.

Endre let out a hiss and glared at the nurse. "You didn't even clean it."

"You'll get over it," she snarked, pulling the needle from him and shoving him away. "Go get one of those shakes right away," Jody ordered gruffly. At least Alicia knew Jody would be there to protect her and this baby with everything she had.

Nora stifled a giggle at the sour face Endre made, and full-on burst out laughing when he glared into the bottle of the meal replacement shake with absolute distaste.

"They're awful, aren't they?" Nora laughed. Alicia laughed right along with her. Served him right.

"My turn, princess?" Zeke questioned, stepping up to Jody. Alicia loved that he thought of her sister like a princess, it was cute.

Her administration of the serum to Zeke was much gentler than the full-on stabbing she used with Endre.

"What are we going to do?" Alicia leaned over and whispered in Jackson's ear from where he'd pulled up a seat next to her.

"I don't know," he admitted with a shrug, "but we'll do it together."

"We're going to have a *baby*," she reminded him.

"And we're going to get married. And we're going to work on a serum for all three of us," he concluded, as if it were that simple. Maybe it *was* that simple.

CHAPTER THIRTY-FIVE

Jody looked around the room at each of the faces she now considered family. Even Endre. Well, maybe not Gustafson, the jury was still out on him and his band of Hunters.

It had been a week since the discovery of her niece or nephew growing in Alicia's womb as well as the administration of the serum to Endre and Zeke. The new formulation performed just as Alicia expected it would. Neither of the men experienced the extreme starvation Nora had and were just as healthy as ever.

Gustafson cleared his throat and the attention of everyone who sat around the table turned toward him. Today was the deadline they'd all agreed to for announcing their plans for the future. Maybe not everyone had a five-year plan laid out, but at least an idea of their immediate futures.

"As per the agreement with Dr. Collins," Gustafson started.

"While you were beating the crap out of him," Alicia mumbled under her breath from beside Jody.

Gustafson continued as if he hadn't heard her, "You were to develop your cure, then produce it for us to distribute to Vampires worldwide. We are at a point where the Hunters need to know what you all plan to do and where you plan to go."

"So you can keep tabs on us?" Endre accused, eyebrows raised.

"Yes," Gustafson replied without hesitation. "We'd like to keep open lines of communication with you. As allies," he amended.

"Right." Zeke scowled at the Hunter.

"Listen," Gustafson urged, leaning forward, an air of sincerity about him, "I grew up learning how to hunt and kill Vampires. So did he." He pointed to Jackson. "It is not easy to change a mindset so ingrained, but we are working on it. We know none of you chose to be Vampires, you've shown us the struggles you endure to fight against your nature. We are faced with the same thing. We were born Hunters. We will always feel the need to hunt, but if we ally with you we can put those instincts to better use by distributing the serum and giving other Vampires a second chance."

"Jackson and I will be staying here, in the lab," Alicia announced, her voice strong and confident. "We'll continue to manufacture the serum as well as continue researching any improvements that can be made to its formulation."

Jody had already suspected that was Alicia's plan; she also knew the unspoken reason for sticking close to the lab was the need to create a new formula for Jackson and their unborn child. Alicia would more than likely require a similar formulation, considering she now carried a piece of Jackson's DNA.

"The Hunters will fund the research," Gustafson revealed to everyone's surprise. "This benefits us all."

"Thank you, that will make things easier, no doubt," Jackson acknowledged.

"We do *request,*" Gustafson continued, emphasizing what he was about to say was not a decree … or he hoped it wouldn't be perceived as one, "Alicia does not continue with her employment."

"I'm pretty sure I don't have a job there anymore," Alicia laughed. "And I imagine I'll be pretty busy here."

Jody could guess she was probably right. They'd all been outside their lives for a month now. She'd at least filed for and was granted a leave of absence from the hospital. Jody hoped the same 'request' wouldn't be asked of her to leave employment.

"You're probably right, but I didn't want to leave it unsaid," Gustafson admitted with a shrug.

"Zeke and I will remain just outside the cities," Jody took her turn to speak, "though we won't be residing in the lab, we will be living at my house nearby. I, however," she added, turning to Gustafson so there was absolutely no question as to whom she was speaking, "will be continuing my employment at the hospital when my leave expires next week."

A little thrill went through her, announcing the co-habitation arrangement Zeke had agreed to. It had been a whirlwind romance from the start with them, and although society's standards dictated their move to living together was too fast, she would argue they weren't exactly part of the average of society any longer. Alicia beamed at her announcement, knowing they wouldn't be far from one another.

"The Hunters' Council has also discussed your employment, and we feel it is in everyone's best interest you continue your nursing work at the hospital," Gustafson agreed, as if what Jody had said had been up for debate of any kind.

"So glad I have your council's permission," she remarked drily.

Gustafson shrugged, as if to say *what can you do?* Jody didn't buy that. She could imagine he'd had some significant impact on the unwanted decisions their *council* was making about their lives. It was a wise move on his part not to tell her what she could and couldn't do. She was neither Vampire nor Hunter, so as far as she was concerned, she didn't fall under the jurisdiction of their policing body. Zeke, however, was a different story.

"What will *you* be doing with your time?" Gustafson's interrogation aimed at Zeke.

Zeke's eyebrows shot up in an expression of surprise. Not that he hadn't thought of what he was going to do—they'd talked about it at length—but Jody was sure the expression was borne of the fact Gustafson demanded an explanation. She supposed it did make sense they would keep tabs on everyone. It was smart in some ways, seeing as they were basically the first test subjects with no long-term studies on the effects of the serum. There could be degradation over time. The affects could wear off. For a group who had spent centuries policing the actions of Vampires, the Hunters would want to know if things changed. In other ways, trying to dictate to Vampires—or former Vampires— how they could live their lives was a dangerous prospect. Thus far, all three Vampires who had taken the serum retained advanced strength and senses even over those of Hunters. They were still lethal if pushed to that point.

"Oh, you know, I planned on sponging off Jody, just hanging out at her house and eating her food," Zeke quipped, giving Gustafson a bored look.

The Hunter at least had the sense to look contrite. "Point taken," he confessed, the corners of his mouth turned down into a frown.

"Since you asked so nicely," Zeke deadpanned, "I will be doing a little of everything. I'm going to fix up the damage at Jody's house from Micelli's goons. Then I'll be around here to help in the lab, doing whatever else Alicia and Jackson need done. We're here to help you guys, with anything," he added, looking pointedly at where Alicia's hands rested over her belly.

"Thank you," Alicia sniffled. "It means a lot to me to know you guys will be close."

"You retiring from rescuing damsels in distress?" Jackson chuckled.

"Nah, I'll do a little of that in between," Zeke admitted with a grin. "Although, I don't have to try to convince any of them to fall in love with me now." He winked at Jody and she couldn't contain the goofy grin spreading across her face.

"What about you?" Alicia asked Nora.

Nora and Endre's plans were what they had all been anticipating hearing. Jody knew they were leaving, but no one knew where they were going or how long they'd be gone. She could do with a break from Endre, but even with his rough edges—which she would have thought should have smoothed out over a few centuries—she was still going to miss him.

"We're going to do a bit of traveling," Nora answered, then quickly added, "but we'll be back for when the baby comes."

"Where are you off to?" Jody found herself asking.

She clamped her mouth shut tight, the question having flown from her mouth unbidden. She figured there was a reason they hadn't offered any specifics yet, and Jody imagined that reason was the hulking Hunter currently staring them down.

"Norway," Endre answered. "Nora has requested to see my birthplace, and as you all seem to be well aware, I cannot refuse a request from my beloved."

He turned to her with a warm smile and Jody swooned a little. Damn that man could be charming when he wanted to be. It was just a damn shame he didn't seem to want to be very often.

"We'll keep in contact … with everyone." Nora shot a pointed look at Gustafson.

"Since I know you will ask, though I feel no obligation to give you one damned piece of information, I will provide you with further specifics to keep you the Hel away from us," Endre sighed, directing his attention to Gustafson. "We leave tonight."

"Good luck to you, then," Gustafson offered, wisely keeping any additional questions to himself.

"We will remain in constant contact with the lab. Believe me when I say if I hear of your Hunters doing anything amiss, I will personally exterminate each and every one of you," Endre threatened in low tones.

"The threat in unnecessary," Gustafson reassured. "We have no intention of making enemies."

"Good. Now, have we sufficiently answered your questions on our planned whereabouts to satisfy your needs?"

"I do believe you have." The Hunter rose from the table with a nod of farewell to each of them before leaving.

"Endre, that was rude. We need to get along with them," Alicia chided, crossing her arms over her chest.

"I will not make it easy for them to keep tabs on us. I am not accountable to them. We will be checking in with you all at frequent intervals to notify you of our current location and the states of health. The Hunters do not need to be made aware of every time I close my eyes and make us an easy target," Endre argued.

"*We're* the ones who will have to deal with them on a day-to-day basis, we don't need to add more conflict to an already tense situation," Alicia told him with a glower.

Scowling, Endre turned to Nora. "Are you sure you like these women? They are both infuriating."

"No more than you, honey," Nora admitted with a saccharine smile and peck on his cheek.

"Touché, lamb," Endre conceded. "It is time we went to rest, we leave in," he turned his new phone to view the time, "three hours."

Nora followed Endre's lead and rose from the table. "Hugs! I need hugs from everyone," she demanded tearfully, pulling Jody from her chair. "Take care of your sister and that little one, we'll see you soon," Nora whispered in her ear.

"You know I will," Jody replied, when Nora relinquished her death-grip and allowed oxygen back into her lungs.

"I'm not hugging you," Endre protested, arms crossed with a scowl on his face.

"I'll miss you, too," Jody told him with a smile.

She really would. What were they going to do without their resident ornery bastard?

Endre grunted, but pulled her into his side in some semblance of an embrace, Jody figured it was as close as he was going to get.

When everyone had embraced, Nora and Endre left for their room, leaving the sisters and their respective men around the table.

Jody turned to Alicia. "I think we should head out, too."

"I figured you'd probably want to get home and sleep in your own bed," Alicia acknowledged. Jody was glad she wasn't upset at their leaving.

Another round of hugs and a sufficient Minnesota good-bye ensued for another ten minutes before Zeke took Jody's hand, bringing it to his mouth for a kiss.

"Shall we be off to your castle, princess?" Zeke asked with a smirk.

"I think we shall," Jody laughed.

The last month had been anything but a fairytale. Nevertheless, Jody was sure she would live as close to happily ever after as she was going to get in this lifetime—especially with her not-so-Vampire knight in shining armor by her side.

Endre let out a deep breath and watched Nora sleep beside him on the plane. The 'cure' they'd all taken wasn't what he had envisioned when he'd set out to create one centuries ago. He'd imagined he would be full-fledged human, but he saw that wasn't plausible. There were changes they'd all undergone in the transition to Vampires that were irreversible. What Alicia had given them had been the best they could hope for. They still retained advantages of a Vampire, such as enhanced senses and strength, but they also retained some weaknesses, such as the sensitivity of light which was the price they paid for the superior vision. But what mattered most was the demon inside them all no longer thirsted for the blood of innocent— or in most cases, not so innocent—humans. Without the monsters whispering atrocities in their ears, Endre retained hope he could live out a semi-normal life with his beloved.

Glancing over at Nora once more, he ensured she was still asleep before pulling the little velvet box from his jacket pocket. The dark garnet shone a deep crimson from between the folds of soft fabric, coaxing Endre to ruin his plans of proposing marriage to his love on the shores of his homeland and wake her to ask now, but he wouldn't give in to its siren call. After all they had been through together, he needed to do this right. He needed to prove he was worthy of the title of husband.

Swiftly stuffing the box back into the depths of his jacket when Nora stirred, Endre pulled her sleeping form closer to him and said a silent prayer of thanks to the gods of old. Never once had he imagined after having risen in his second life that he would have the opportunity for happiness, and yet, here Nora was beside him. The gods of his ancestors had deemed him worthy of such a rare blessing and he would do everything in his power to ensure he didn't fuck it up.

EPILOGUE

"Seriously, if you move that cake one more time, I am going to slap you. It is just fine where it's at," Jody scolded Alicia.

"You'd slap the pregnant woman?" Alicia questioned in exaggerated surprise, pushing out her gigantic baby bump for emphasis.

Alicia knew damned well her sister wouldn't slap her, but the glower she got from her in response was well worth the teasing.

"I don't give a damn if it's your baby shower," Jody ranted, "you've moved that cake fifteen times! Leave it there and find something else to do. Go sit down. Go relax or something."

"Don't be ridiculous," Jackson countered, pecking Alicia on the cheek before leading her over to a chair. "It's only been moved twelve times."

A resounding smack, which echoed off the brick of the enclosed courtyard, drew a hearty laugh from Jackson. "You're supposed to be on *my* side!" Alicia protested.

"Oh my God!" a gasp sounded from the door, drawing Alicia's attention to Nora standing there. "You look so—"

"Gigantic? Enormous? Whale-like?" Alicia finished for her.

"I was going to say adorable," Nora laughed, pulling her into a hug.

"Do you see how huge this thing is?" Alicia pointed down to the round protrusion. "And there are still three months to go."

"She's being dramatic." Rolling her eyes, Jody enveloped Nora in a bear-hug. "I'm so glad you guys made it back in time."

"We wouldn't miss the baby shower," Nora protested indignantly. "Well, Endre would have if I let him. You know how he is."

"He can hear you," Endre sighed, plucking a beer from the cooler next to the little table. "Is it really proper etiquette to have alcohol at a baby shower?" he asked, twisting the cap off his beer and taking a swig, his concerns about etiquette apparently forgotten already.

"There aren't any kids here … yet. I can't drink it anyway, and Jackson says he didn't want any." Alicia shrugged.

They had an overabundance of burgers and brats, standard outdoor party fare, to go with the beer and pop. Jody had questioned her sanity when she wanted to have a picnic in the daytime for the shower, but Alicia really wanted to feel a little bit normal again. Their new extended family, in the form of nearly two-dozen Hunters, had kindly put up canopies shading the whole courtyard, and paired with really dark tinted sunglasses, she hardly had to squint.

"Everything looks great," Nora gushed, surveying the setup.

Alicia had been so excited about seeing Nora again—and Endre, too, she guessed—she may have gone overboard. At least that's what Jackson and Jody kept telling her.

"How's the little one doing?" Nora asked, snagging a beer for herself. "Are you ever going to tell us if it's a boy or a girl?"

"I'm the only one who knows," Jody taunted in a sing-songy voice. "We're revealing the sex today. With this!" Jody presented a black balloon covered in pink and blue question marks.

"I don't understand," Endre puzzled, shaking his head at the balloon.

"Man, neither do I," Zeke sighed, walking past with a tray full of meat.

"Did you get my—" Alicia started.

"Yes, woman! For the love of all that is holy, he got your damned blood," Jody groaned, looking to the sky for guidance of some kind. "She's driving me insane," she said, turning to Nora.

"Will someone explain this balloon?" Endre prompted.

"There are pieces of either pink or blue paper inside, and when she pops the balloon, we'll know whether the baby is a boy or girl," Nora explained patiently to the very confused Endre.

"Food's done!" Jackson announced to the growing crowd.

Alicia hadn't realized when she started planning the party that thirty people—mostly men who eat a whole helluva lot—meant she'd practically have to buy out the meat section of the grocery store. But it was worth it to have everyone together again. Everyone milled around, eating and drinking. Some of the Hunters retreated to a corner where they'd set up a horseshoe pit and corn bag toss. Others mingled with the Vampires and former Vampires, regaling tales of hunting down less than willing Vampires along with stories of being sought out for the serum.

The last few months had been interesting to say the least. Not only were Alicia and Jackson still getting used to the idea of their growing family, but they'd spent every spare waking moment producing vials of the serum for the Hunters to distribute. Alicia knew eventually they'd get to making the serum to take away the blood cravings for the three of them—her, Jackson and baby V, as they'd dubbed their little guy or girl— but she still felt like she was behind.

"All in good time," Jackson whispered, rubbing Alicia's shoulders.

"I hate when you do that," she groaned, dropping her head forward and enjoying his firm hands kneading sore muscles.

"Then I'll stop," he replied, the wonderful massage ceasing.

Alicia didn't have to see him to hear the smile in his voice. *Smartass*.

"No, not that," she huffed, "the mind-reading thing."

"It's not mind reading when you make the same face every time you think about how disappointed you are with our progress," Jackson said, kissing the top of her head and continuing the massage. "We have time."

"I know, I just wanted to have it figured out before a wedding and a baby," Alicia sighed with a shrug.

"I would think you'd have learned by now plans don't always happen the way we want just because we make them," her wonderful fiancé wisely told her.

"I know." She turned her face to catch the kiss Jackson was about to plant on her head with her lips.

"Are you guys ready?" Jody prompted, rushing up with the looming black balloon. It would have been ominous if not for the pastel question marks.

"Remember, it doesn't matter if it's a boy or girl," Jackson reminded her, "despite whatever plans you've already made in that head of yours."

"I know," Alicia acknowledged with a nod.

She actually didn't have a preference one way or the other on the sex of the baby. Some people just said that, but Alicia honestly didn't care which as long as the baby was healthy and didn't try to eat her.

"We're ready," Jackson announced to her sister.

Jody let out a squeal and bounced around excitedly. "Just so you know, keeping this a secret has

~ 275 ~

been *killing* me! Come on." She pulled Alicia to the center of the courtyard, Jackson trailing not far behind.

"Is it time?" Nora shouted, rushing over to the growing ring of bodies around them.

Alicia looked around at all the happy, smiling faces, still completely floored at the gathering of people around them. Jody arranged her and Jackson in the center of the circle of people, the balloon floating between them. With a ceremonial flourish of her arm, Jody handed Alicia a pin.

"We all know why we're here," Jody announced to the crowd, "and only part of it is the beer." A chuckle went through the crowd. "But seriously, I know Alicia and Jackson are touched by the support of everyone here and how we've all come together as more than allies. We've come together as a community, albeit a strange one, with a common goal. Today our community is whole again with Endre and Nora joining us, but I think we all know there's more work to be done and there will be things that will separate us in the future for one reason or another. So, let's celebrate the reunion of our little family, however brief it may be, and find out what color clothes we're going to spoil this kid with!"

A round of applause accompanied by whistles and cheers sounded from the crowd. Jody took a little bow and waved the attention over—Vanna White style—to where Alicia and Jackson waited with the balloon.

"Should we count down or something?" Jackson asked Jody the Party Planner.

"No! Just pop the damn thing, we're all dying of suspense over here," she yelled back.

With a deep breath, Alicia plunged the pin into the balloon and was instantly covered in pink confetti. A cheer went through the group. Alicia looked over to Jackson, pink bits of paper stuck on his shirt and in his hair.

"We're having a girl?" he gasped, a gigantic smile on his face.

"Looks like it!" Alicia announced, leaping into his arms.

Jackson pressed light kisses to her lips that turned decidedly less sweet and should be relegated to the bedroom.

"Congratulations," Gustafson's voice broke into their make-out session.

"Thanks," Jackson accepted, a little breathlessly as he grasped the Hunter's outstretched hand.

"Got any names picked out?" he inquired.

"I was thinking Bella," Alicia said.

"No. No preexisting Vampire names," Jackson contradicted.

"Alice?"

"No."

"Rosalee?"

"No, Alicia."

"Elena?"

All she got that time was a stern look.

"Akasha?"

"Alicia," Jackson said in warning.

"Fine, fine, fine," Alicia sighed. "Violet." When Jackson gave her a sour look she added, "I'm actually serious about that one."

"We'll see," Jackson said, conceding nothing.

THE END

AUTHOR'S NOTE

Irreversible marks the conclusion of The Bloodlust Chronicles, and I have to admit I'm sad to see it end. Irresistible was the first book I ever published, and I will always be grateful to those who helped me along in the journey. I learned along the way that putting out a book isn't just about getting the words down on paper. There is so much that goes into it, and so many people involved along the way. It may be the end of The Bloodlust Chronicles, but you all will continue to see more writing from me. Onward to new and exciting things, I say! Armed with my ever-increasing knowledge of the book world, I plan to breathe life into a whole host of story ideas stacking up in the dozen or so notebooks scattered throughout my house.

TARA IS A WICKEDLY TALENTED WRITER WHO LIVES IN THE FROZEN NORTH IN MINNESOTA WITH HER WONDERFUL HUSBAND AND TWO RAMBUNCTIOUS LITTLE DUDES. SHE IS AN ENGINEER DURING THE DAY, A CRAZY MOM IN THE AFTERNOON AND A WRITER AT NIGHT. SHE ENJOYS SPENDING HER TIME PLAYING IN THE DIRT WHEN HER GARDENS AREN'T COVERED IN SNOW AND LISTENING TO A WIDE VARIETY OF MUSIC THAT INSPIRES HER WRITING — SOMETIMES DOING BOTH AT THE SAME TIME.

Contact Tara

- Email -
TaraVasser.Author@gmail.com

- Facebook —
www.facebook.com/TaraVasserAuthor

- Website —
http://www.AuthorTaraVasser.com

- Twitter -
www.twitter.com/TaraVasser

- Goodreads -
www.goodreads.com/author/show/153
25170.Tara_Vasser

Other Books By Tara

The Bloodlust Chronicles
Irresistible – Book 1
Irredeemable – Book 2
Irreplaceable – Book 3
Irrecoverable – Book 4
Irrepressible – Book 5
Irreversible – Book 6
Irrevocable – Book 7